The Inn Closes for Christmas and Other Dark Tales

The Inn Closes for Christmas and Other Dark Tales

Cledwyn Hughes

BASKERVILLE

An imprint of JOHN MURRAY

The Inn Closes for Christmas first published in USA in 1947
as 'He Dared Not Look Behind' by A. A. Wyn
The Inn Closes for Christmas first published in Great Britain in
1947 as 'The Inn Closes for Christmas' by The Pilot Press
'Only a Green Shutter' first published in 1959 in
Home magazine, Fleetway Publications
'The Hedgehog' first published in 1946 in *Celtic Story*,
Aled Vaughan (ed.), Pendulum Publications

This edition first published in 2025 by Baskerville
An imprint of John Murray (Publishers)

1

A CIP catalogue record for this title is available from the British Library

Hardback ISBN 9781399827645
ebook ISBN 9781399827652

Typeset in Sabon MT by Hewer Text UK Ltd, Edinburgh
Printed and bound in Great Britain by Clays Ltd, Elcograf S.p.A.

John Murray policy is to use papers that are natural, renewable and
recyclable products and made from wood grown in sustainable forests.
The logging and manufacturing processes are expected to conform
to the environmental regulations of the country of origin.

Carmelite House
50 Victoria Embankment
London EC4Y 0DZ

www.johnmurraypress.co.uk

John Murray Press, part of Hodder & Stoughton Limited
An Hachette UK company

The authorised representative in the EEA is Hachette Ireland, 8 Castlecourt
Centre, Dublin 15, D15 XTP3, Ireland (email: info@hbgi.ie)

Contents

The Inn Closes for Christmas

In thoughts from the
visions of the night,
when deep sleep falleth
on men.

The Book of Job

The First Papers

I

The bank manager, as he had done for so many Christmases now, opened the file. As he had done each Boxing Day for the last ten years. And as always, as he opened it he wondered why he must do this each year. But he seemed driven to it. For the man had asked him that he should do this every Christmas for as long as he should live. Why he, of all men?

Just an ordinary square box file it was. The grey outer cardboard wearing off a little now and showing the brown yellow of the lower layers.

Inside the file a bundle of papers held down by a strong steel spring.

The manager snapped back the spring.

The top papers were in his own handwriting.

Why had he stopped writing it out? After so few pages too.

It would have made a good story, all written out properly . . .

Mrs Sterrill had a wooden leg. But it wasn't really wooden. It was an affair of gleaming chromium and smooth working joints, supple and strong. But it was an artificial limb and although Mrs Sterrill had her one soft shapely leg the other mechanical one didn't quite match. It seemed too shapely, especially at the ankle. And although Mrs Sterrill always wore the most sheer of stockings the difference in the two legs was always plain to see.

Mrs Sterrill was young, twenty-seven, dark-haired and pretty. She was the wife of the only dentist in Welton. And, in spite of her disability, the prettiest and one of the best-dressed women in this little market town. Men would watch her as she drank her Saturday-night cocktail with her husband at the big ivy-covered Arms in the market square. Would watch her with admiration. And only shake their heads sadly as she would get up to walk, leaning heavy on her little husband and moving along slowly.

Mrs Sterrill had lost her leg one year after she had married her dentist husband. Their little green sports car had skidded when rounding a corner and there had been the smash. He had been driving . . .

Straight away that night they had operated and cut off her leg. For weeks she had been in bed. For a long time she had walked with crutches until they had supplied her with the artificial limb.

People had talked and shaken their heads. Said how very sad it was that she should lose her leg when so young. How very sad and so much the worse for a woman. But lucky they said that it wasn't one of *his hands*. Where would a dentist be without his hands?

For he was quite a good dentist was Mr Sterrill. Two years older than his wife, with dark moustache and wavy black hair. And those strong white hands with the thick short hairy fingers.

They lived in a biggish house near to the traffic lights in the centre of the town. A gay house with the outside painted cream and with green window boxes, always masses of flowers. The brown varnished front door with the brightly polished brass knocker, and the two little bell-pushes, the one labelled DAY. The other NIGHT. To the right of the door was set Mr Sterrill's plate. His name in white letters on a brown background. *William Sterrill, Dental Surgeon*.

Young and prosperous Mr Sterrill. The only dentist in the town. His wife charming and good-looking.

The only thing which could mar their happiness was her artificial leg. But they both seemed to forget it. And people watching said what a devoted couple they were. He so kind to her in her affliction. And she so patient and bearing it all so well.

Yes, to the people of Welton, the world of the Sterrills seemed quite bright in spite of the leg.

But one morning the news went around the town. Went quickly around the town, as such news does in such places.

For Mrs Sterrill had been found dead.

How did she die?

It was all very interesting and rather terrible.

II

Next in the file a small bundle of newspaper cuttings. Taken from the Welton local newspaper of ten years ago. The whole clipped together by a bulldog paper clip, the bright steel of the handles beginning to rust a little.

The headlines of the cuttings had been cut away, the date written on in ink, and the paper was going a little yellow with the years. Delicately the bank manager held each cutting in his long thin white fingers as he read it.

The First Cutting

I, police constable Thomas Tulle was called from the police station by Mr Sterrill of 3, High Street, Welton, on November the first. Mr Sterrill arrived at the station on a bicycle. He was fully dressed but under his brown tweed overcoat I could see that he had on a white jacket. His hands were shaking and as he took off his gloves he said:

'Doreen is dead.'

'Come, sir,' I said. 'Pull yourself together. Take a seat.'

He sat down and started to pull on his gloves again.

'Now, sir,' I said, 'Let's hear what you've come to see us about.'

'Doreen, my wife, is dead.'

'Dead, then would it not have been better to have gone to the doctor's first, Mr Sterrill, instead of coming here?'

'I've telephoned the doctor. He's there. He said that I'd better come along and tell you up here, so as to have things right.'

Well, by now I could see that Mrs Sterrill must indeed be dead and that I'd better go along quickly to High Street.

The doctor's car was outside the house.

We went inside. The door leading off the hall to the dental surgery was open. We went into that room, for Dr Pathlabe was there and he called us in.

'Tell us what the room was like,' said the coroner.

It was a little room, sir, panelled in white with the windows facing out over the High Street. The windows covered over with a sort of gauze netting stuff. The usual dental instruments about the room. A small cupboard with glass doors and chromium forceps and syringes inside. Small bottles and the usual smell of such places. And the dental chair.

In the chair was Mrs Sterrill. She was hanging over the one arm of the chair, sir. Her one leg was all doubled up and crooked awkwardly just like a normal leg is after it's been broken.

She was wearing a coloured housecoat. Her hair was done up with a bright ribbon at the back. Around her neck was draped the little serviette, very white, that dentists use to stop the splashing blood.

Dr Pathlabe told us she was dead.

Mr Sterrill went out into the hall as I went across to look at the face of his wife.

It was all twisted and drawn to the one side, the jaws clenched tightly together and with frothy foam at the mouth. It looked terrible, sir, just like somebody when they gnash their teeth in temper. Her face was set like that. I've seen many deaths but nothing quite like that face.

Dr Pathlabe told me to fetch the Inspector. So I did. And when he came he sent for the photographer and he came and took photos. After that we moved her out and to the mortuary up at the hospital.

The coroner spoke to his jury. 'You will note that Mrs Sterrill died this morning. That she died in her husband's dental chair. That she had a white serviette around her throat. That her face was contorted terribly. That her husband went to the police and that Mr Sterrill was greatly upset by the death of his wife. That the Inspector of Police came and was sufficiently impressed to get a photograph of the body taken in the position in which she had died.'

From another paper the next cutting, the paper slightly whiter, the headlines still on.

The Second Cutting

STATEMENT OF MR STERRILL
AT OPENING OF INQUEST

My wife had a lower molar which was abscessed and with the pulp canal gangrenous. She had allowed this to develop without telling me anything about it. But on the morning of the day before she died she told me. I inspected the tooth and put a dressing on it to ease the pain and reduce the inflammation. The next day I decided to try out a new technique for the treatment of such teeth. Briefly it was this. I intended to clean out the cavity and the pulp canal with needles. Then to flush out with peroxide of hundred-volumes strength followed by sodium hypochlorite solution alternately. Then to dry off with paper points. When the cavity was cleared, I intended to fill it with distilled water and then introduce one of the sulphanilamide drugs until the solution was saturated. Then I intended to put in a temporary filling. Now, according to professional reports there was every indication that this treatment would reduce the abscess and destroy all the infection. If necessary I intended to put on another dressing at the end of the week.

When my wife came to the surgery it was about half past ten. I noticed that her hands were trembling and that her face was flushed. She also complained that she felt very tired. Also all that day she had been tired.

Naturally I put this down to the pain from the tooth and the anxiety at the thought of the minor operation.

When she opened her mouth she complained that her jaws felt stiff. I noticed, too, that her tongue seemed to be pulled to the one side. I assumed this was the result of the pain in the lower jaw and the inflammation which was still there in spite of the previous day's dressing.

It was after I had painted the gums that she complained of severe pain in the limbs. I thought that she was joking and carried on with the procedure up to the point of clear-ing out the socket and flooding the cavity with distilled water. It was then that she said the pain in her limbs had become very severe. I then stopped working and she said that she felt very cold and then very hot. Soon after this her jaws became locked and her face distorted. She went then into convulsions and quickly died.

I phoned Dr Pathlabe and he quickly came, and when he saw my wife he sent me up to the police station.

I have to assume that my wife died of acute tetanus infection. Recollecting back, I recall that she tore the skin of her hand while tidying up one of the window boxes upstairs a few days ago. I can only assume that she caught a tetanus infection from the soil, which entered her system by way of the injury to her hand. Probably the symptoms I recall during the time before her death were due to the tetanus infection and not, as I had supposed, to the infected tooth. The tetanus infection must have reached its climax when she was in the chair, and there she died.

The third cutting must have been at one time in the same report as the one given above. But it had been cut away and on the top had been pasted a small label. A label with a black heavy line around the edge, such as profes-sional people use for labelling bottles of drugs, etc. Across the label was carefully printed, REPORT OF PATHOLOGIST.

The Third Cutting

I was called to the house of Mr Sterrill by telephone. He said something over the phone to the effect that his wife was ill, very ill. He mentioned, too, that it looked like tetanus and so I packed in my case some phials of anti-tetanus serum which I always kept in my kitchen refrigerator.

I arrived at the house and was shown in by Mr Sterrill to the surgery. He seemed very nervous and excited and when we entered the room he just pointed to the chair and said, 'She's dead!'

I went across and examined her. I checked her heart and her pupil reactions and by other conclusive medical tests ascertained that Mrs Sterrill was indeed dead.

Her body was twisted to the one side, half hanging over the leather arm of the chair. Her one hand was holding very tightly a small fold of her housecoat which she seemed to have gathered up in her palm. Her artificial limb was twisted to the one side and on later examination I found that the stump had become quite detached from the socket of the limb. Her whole body was tight and taut. Her face was drawn and twisted, and with the jaw muscles firmly fixed the tongue almost bitten through.

On the thumb of her right hand was a small bruise and the skin was punctured. The whole thumb seemed to be swollen slightly, although the limb did not seem to have the usual measure of inflammation present in this type of tetanus infection. For my first diagnosis was that Mrs

Sterrill had died from tetanus, or what is more commonly known as 'lock-jaw'.

Mr Sterrill informed the police on my suggestion. The body was removed to the hospital where I performed a post-mortem. The PM confirmed that Mrs Sterrill had indeed died of tetanus infection.

III

The last cutting was a very small one. The Bank Manager held it flat in his palm as he read it.

The Last Cutting

FUNERAL OF MRS STERRILL
Mrs Sterrill of 3, High Street, Welton, was buried yesterday in the churchyard of St Judes. As recorded elsewhere a verdict of accidental death was given at the Inquest. The service . . .

That was all.

The rest of the papers in the file were fastened together with a length of brown advertising twine, with the name of some small village stores on it. The manager undid the bow of the string and opened out the papers.

There were many papers, all written in a neat handwriting on a blue, expensive notepaper. The first page had the simple words, written in large letters with a red pencil:
THE CONFESSION OF WILLIAM STERRILL

The bank manager looked at the first page a few moments before starting to read the inside sheets.

It always read as new, those mad words from that little dentist . . .

What Mr Sterrill Wrote

I

My life has known much fear.

Much in my early days at school. In the small school on the side of the hill in Wales, in the village where my father had been vicar. It was a boarding school and I was the only day boy there, pushed in on account of my father's influence. The boys mostly the sons of well-to-do parents. Some with their fathers away in India. Who sent their sons to this school in the mountains where the advert said that there was plenty of fresh air and fresher food. In that school I was nicknamed the Day Boy. But after a time that became stale as another day boy arrived, and so afterwards I was called Prayer Book in honour of my reverend father. And that name followed me throughout the school until I reached the Sixth Form, and by then I was known as just PB. I answered like a well-trained dog to that name. The time was once when the games master had called me PB when he had forgotten my name, William Sterrill.

The boy who was always afraid.

Afraid of doing my homework in case the others hadn't done it, for then I would be a traitor. Afraid of not doing my homework for then I would be in disgrace and get punishment. I seldom played games. The fear of being floored at football and the hard ball at cricket were always with me. And when they forced me to play football all the other boys would kick me and the games master would never blow the whistle and call foul.

Examinations didn't worry me so much. I could pass them easily although I seldom swotted.

When I started in that school my fear was evident. My eyes would move right and left. 'Shifty' that's what one master called me once. But by the time I left the school my fear was turned around and buried deep inside me. There it seemed to ferment and there were days when it frothed up from the hard core that was always there. Frothed up and almost bubbled over. So that it was hard and difficult to stay and not run away. To run away from nothing . . .

I knew that it would be useless to run for I would only carry it with me.

And so it was harder to bear on the last day of school than the first. My fear was deep inside me. No master could readily say 'That boy is afraid,' or one of the boys say 'Old PB is scared stiff.' But I knew that my fear was buried so deep that it would take a long time to get it out of me. It would always be with me, no matter if I ran or stayed.

II

And then came the days at college. For the first two years my life was misery. For I worried about one thing only. The day when I would have to do my first extraction, take out the first tooth of my first patient. The other dental students laughed and never worried about this thing. They always said, leave the patient to worry. It's much more his worry, they said.

The fear took me in strange ways. I would look at my hands. Would they be firm and strong enough? Would I fumble? Would the patient scream? What if it should be an old woman or worse, a small young child? What if septicaemia should set in? Supposing the patient should die? A coroner's court. Manslaughter. Jail. My name never to be on the dental register.

As I lay on my hard bed in my lodgings I thought all these things. I saw disgrace and failure because I fumbled with the first real tooth I touched.

Much more than examinations it worried me.

And the night before I had to do my first practical at the out-patients clinic was the hell of those early days. But nothing to what has been of late . . .

Even now, after all the thousands of extractions I have done, every time I perform this operation the memory of that night comes back to me. Comes back to me as I fill the syringe and place the curved forceps on the sterile tray.

The night before, I walked the streets of the city. Out into the park and down by the broad wide river to watch the ships moving out on the night tide. The lights at the holiday resort opposite the great northern port. The clang of the bell buoys, and the bottles and wood hobby-horsing along on the water as they were swept out to sea on the fast-moving water.

I walked the park. I stood by the river. The sun was rising as I turned in, creeping over the steep roofs of the tenement houses. I slept all the morning and through into the early afternoon. And there was, of course, the dream, thousands of mouths opening. And in each just one decayed tooth. And as I reached in to extract, the tooth would suddenly become sound and it would be the next tooth that was rotten. And as I changed my hold to that one, it, too, would become sound and healthy. And so on as I reached in. Until I dreamt that they gave me a special forceps with wide ends like the ends of two sharp pointed garden rakes coming together. They gave me this tool which would take out a whole row of teeth. They laughed as they gave it to me and said, try this. But I remember that in my dream I was glad to have it. And how it ripped a whole row of teeth from their sockets. But even with this tool all was not well. For new teeth seemed to sprout to take the place of those I had extracted with my wonderful tool.

But I survived my practical. The patient was an old docker. He said, 'Do your stuff, lad, and never mind me.'

And so all was well.

III

You'll get a wife easy, old man, they said. Easy for a good-looking guy like you.

But somehow it was not quite like that. No woman seemed to stay. And for a time it obsessed me and I kept asking each fresh girl, do you love me, do you love me, do you love . . . until they got tired of saying yes, yes, yes and in the end said, I don't think it'll work, Bill. And I could see my life. My death as a lonely old man, unloved in life. Unmourned in death.

And then Doreen came along. She was all I ever wanted. Her father had been a clergyman, he was now dead. Her mother was dying of cancer. She was too ill to come to our wedding. By the time we came back from our honeymoon she, too, was gone.

Doreen was all mine.

What I had always wanted. A woman of my own.

And we were very happy. For although she was very attractive, yet I was the only man in her life.

Those first two years when I was building up the

practice in Welton, those happy days. And when my rival retired and I bought his practice, all seemed well and a lifetime of happiness assured.

Until.

IV

The memory of that night stays with me. For then all started.

It was moonlight and the little sports car roared along the narrow road running parallel with the river out of Welton. The water on the one side. On the other the big rounded dark trunks of the beech trees. The moon shining full in October, and Doreen saying how lovely the hunter moon was. The black stripes of the shadows of the trees mushrooming out into the black mass of leafy shadow. The Mill House above the weir reflecting clear its lighted windows yellow in the water. Two years then we had been married. We'd been out to the cinema in the town next to Welton. And now, home. Doreen by my side wrapped deep in her fur coat, she'd just had it I remember. Bought in memory of our wedding anniversary. Her elbow nudged deep into the hollow of my groin. The sprung steering wheel vibrating softly in my hand.

I still don't remember how it happened. I know there was a cat. Running from the bright moonlight into the dark shadows. I swerved to avoid it. Doreen's hand came out of her pocket and clutched my knee. And then came the skid. They said afterwards that it was the fallen leaves of autumn. Decayed, slimy and slippery on the road surface. The leaves from the wonderful beeches. I felt the car slipping and I twisted and turned the wheel trying to steer into the skid. But our car still slipped fast sideways. If only we could crush in between one of those many trunks we might have a chance. The hedges and the field would be softer.

It was the side on which Doreen was sitting that hit the solid tree trunk. The last tree in the row, just below the bridge.

She screamed.

I had been in hospital three days before they told me about her.

How they had had to amputate.

No chance to save that slim graceful right leg of hers.

It was the young house surgeon at the city hospital who told me. His young face a little troubled and unhardened yet with the years of practice. But she'll walk he said. She'll walk all right. They're very clever now.

Odd the first thought I had when he told me.

That little hard corn on her little toe.

She would miss it.

V

In the days that followed I was still afraid. Afraid to look behind as I pushed Doreen along in the invalid chair. For perhaps they may be looking, with pity or disgust. Perhaps pointing.

And when Doreen moved to crutches and we walked slowly together up the High Street people would move far aside to give us room to pass. Doreen with the wide arc of her crutches.

But through all this I loved Doreen.

Until . . .

Until the day when they fitted her with an artificial limb.

It was March when we went again to the city in the hired car. For I had said that I would never drive again.

A cold windy March day with men in mufflers and the street lads with small drops of water dangling on the ends of their noses.

Gently I carried Doreen into the taxi. And at the end of the journey helped her out again, outside the offices of the limb company.

One of the first things they told us was that it would cost about eighty pounds. Would it be all right? I just nodded. Then they mentioned a spare. Doreen said no, I can always use my crutches if anything should happen to the thing.

How long was it since the stump had hardened and had the surgeon said that it would be in order to be fitted with an artificial limb?

We told them that all was in order and while I sat watching they started. The two young women in their white coats among the glass shelves and the chromium stands. The trial pieces and the measuring tapes. At last they tried on a trial limb. The one girl making notes. The other adjusting the screws and the tapes.

It was the straps that hurt me most. Encircling the waist and high up over the shoulder, so that when she walked she could swing the leg along by rolling her body high and to the one side. They measured her sound leg too and made a model of that. To get near to the same shape as possible they said. But we're afraid that we can never quite match the real leg, they said. The shape of the one sound leg alters so much as a woman gets older. Especially when she has only one.

It's more important that the leg should be comfortable than that it should look pretty they said.

We agreed.

Anything if Doreen might walk again. If only to hobble.

You'll be able to walk fine they said. It's lucky you have so much of a stump left. They talked much of stumps and straps. Aluminium and alloys.

We just kept on nodding.

Then they mentioned special shoes.

Doreen took notice at that. Shan't I ever be able to wear nice shoes again, ever?

They soothed her. Yes, of course. Only madam, it's like this. The one shoe will wear out much more quickly than the other. And we arrange to have the one shoe duplicated. So that when repairs are carried out you won't be in need of shoes. We have many designs in all the latest styles.

They showed us the catalogue.

VI

They brought it one morning just after breakfast. Two men brought it from the station.

A long and narrow box. Labelled, *With Great Care.* FOR MEDICAL USE.

Doreen and I looked at it as it lay there in the hall under the rows of coats and hats.

'Shall I unpack it?' I said.

She leaned on her one crutch as I carried the box in my arms and through into the kitchen and laid it on the table. Then she sat down and watched me as I unpacked the case, wrenching the top off with the claw end of the hammer from the toolbox.

First came the sawdust and the sheets of corrugated paper.

The thing itself was wrapped in many lengths of tissue paper. Like orchids, or some precious stone.

Doreen had got up now and was sitting on the edge of the table, her sound leg dangling over the side. She helped with her own hands to uncover the last layers of paper.

At last came the leg itself shining in the morning sunlight with the straps neatly buckled and folded at the top and the little smear of oil at the joints.

Her first words were: 'Isn't it wonderful, Bill? Now I'll be able to walk again.'

Myself, I hated the thing right then as it lay there, smug in its box. Such a poor substitute, cold and grey, for the rich life of leg that had once been.

But it would enable her to walk. She could go out again without the crutches. She could go out shopping. To the pictures without the worry of having to park her crutches. She could go out for a drink. Lots of things she could do now . . .

I took it out from its box and stood it up on the table.

'Let's try it for shape, Doreen.'

She placed it by the side of her own leg, lifting up her skirt.

I stood back a little and looked at the difference.

'How is it, Bill, how is it?'

I shook my head. Said how it was much fuller than yours darling. And that the curves somehow were all wrong.

'But remember, Bill,' and her voice was anxious, 'Remember what they said about a woman's leg altering with the years.'

'But, darling, it does look artificial. It does look artificial.'

'But, Bill, I'll be able to get about to walk. It's better than no leg at all. And perhaps with decent shoes and stockings it won't look so bad, Bill.'

I agreed with her. But somehow even then I could never believe that it would ever look decent. I knew that no matter where she went men would look at her, my Doreen.

Her lovely face, a little lined now, but still very lovely. They would look at her. Look again. How wonderful she was when she sat. But when she walked. What a shame, what a bloody shame. She's got a gammy leg, man, a gammy leg. And then the talk would pass from legs to other things. Dirty talk, perhaps, arising from my wife's artificial leg.

I knew that this thing of metal, cunningly contrived and so very expensive, I knew that it would be worse, far worse than the nothingness that was there now . . .

VII

And so my wife had to learn to walk all over again. It was strange to see her tottering and grasping around the kitchen and the dining room.

Sometimes when she had been sitting reading or listening to the radio she would forget about her artificial limb. Think that her two legs were sound and she would get up and try to walk. And then she would fall heavily on her face or stumble. Do you wonder that in those days I first came to hate that thing of smooth metal and flexing joints?

For it was worse than learning to walk. For her one sound leg knew the way. But with the other limb she had to learn a new pose, a new stance, a new technique. I helped her all I could. I knew it was only her pride which kept her from throwing away the thing. Her pride, because she knew that if she gave in the only way she could move around was on crutches. And she feared that.

Falling and stumbling. And always she was afraid that she might dent or damage the thing. The thing which had cost so much, more even than we had paid for the little second-hand sports car. Now lying in the yard behind the garage at the bottom of High Street.

In those days I think that some of my fear walked across and stood by Doreen. For she was afraid. Dreadfully afraid that she would have to go about Welton on crutches. And if fear went from me another demon came to take its place. I learned to hate.

To hate that thing which dangled from her. The thing which stood so cold and erect by the side of our bed each night.

VIII

Yes, in those days my fear turned to hate. Hatred of that thing.

Doreen now had a phantom limb. In the night she would cry out and say that her leg was hurting. Her right leg she would say. Rub it, Bill. Rub it. I would reach out to it. But there was no leg there.

We told the surgeon about it. He laughed and said that's a common thing with anybody who's lost a limb. It's what they call a '*phantom limb*'.

Sometimes, too, she would get the pain in the daytime. And then if I was not working on a patient she would call me from the surgery. And then I would have to rub the thing of metal which took the place of her own lost leg. And as I rubbed it I could see the relief in her face and she would whisper.

'Bill, it's like as if it's real.'

But to me who had no cut nerves or severed muscles it seemed wrong and terrible. That she should give life in this way to this thing and make it alive.

IX

But the phantom limb was only the one of Doreen's many problems. She had many.

Shoes were difficult to obtain in the many sizes and shapes and colours dear to the heart of a woman. And then there were the stockings. The metal of the limb seemed to wear out even the best silk much faster than did flesh. And then too it was difficult to suspend the stocking on the new limb, what with the straps and the harness. And so she took to wearing slacks. She had a favourite pair of velvet red. And there were times when I almost forgot that under the softness of the cord there was not warm gentle human flesh, full of life and feeling.

One evening of those days the cat was sitting on her knee. A black soft sleeping thing it was, lazy and slow to move. Yet always, like all cats, with so much hidden activity almost showing beneath the placid surface.

In the lamplight of the lounge it was affectionate and fond. And Doreen used to nurse it on her knee, pet it and stroke the long black hair flat to the body.

I don't know what made Doreen do it. A sudden urge for movement or just curiosity perhaps. But as the cat was resting on the velvet cover of the artificial leg, Doreen suddenly pulled its tail. The cat gave a loud squawk and dug its claws into what it believed was flesh. But its claws rasped against metal with a metallic screech. The cat leapt with a mew from off her knee and into the blackness underneath the couch.

Nothing which Doreen could do would persuade it to come out again.

X

Doreen came to love that leg.

Yes, she came to *love* it.

To love it as if it were a part of her. But more than that. She came to love her union with it. As if it were her lover.

I could see it quite plainly. And when I told her about it she laughed and said that I was crazy to think such a thing. Why, her only lover was me, me her darling husband.

And the way she said that almost made me feel as if that were true. As if that thing meant nothing to her. Was not joined to her by any stronger ties than those of straps and fittings. As a something which helped her to walk, a mere convenience.

I *would* have believed that.

But then she started to take the thing to bed with her.

You might wonder.

I did.

Until I realised that she really loved that leg of hers.

But she was clever.

The excuses she made were clever. Wonderfully, wonderfully clever.

She said that she had grown so used to it that she felt lost without it. That it took her an hour in the morning when she first put it on, to get used to it. That there was all the trouble of strapping and unstrapping. And when I talked to her about patience and that I would help her, she laughed and said that it was she who had to wear the limb.

When I argued she said that the surgeon had said that she was to wear it as much as possible.

But in bed, I said, *in bed*.

'Why not,' she said. 'I can't see anything wrong if it makes me more comfortable.'

And so I had to give in.

But I took to sleeping on her left side so that I should be as far away from it as possible.

I knew when she first took it to bed that a battle was starting.

It was me or the leg.

For she could not love us both.

XI

With the months that passed Doreen came to love the leg. It ceased to be a hindrance. It became a part of her.

And it became a part of me too.

I lived two lives.

The normal life of Mr Sterrill, the dentist.

And then there was my dream life. That became real. So real that every night I was afraid to sleep.

The old fear that I had known so strong in my younger days came slowly back.

I worked by habit.

Doreen guessed and I think knew something of my dreams. I cried out sometimes in my sleep and in the morning she would ask me had I been dreaming? Did I remember calling out in the night? I always said no, nothing.

For in each of those dreams there was one thing – the leg.

XII

The first few dreams about the leg were not so terrifying. But the leg was always the centre of the dream.

Sometimes I would see the leg on a pedestal, perched high and looking so graceful, bathed in a soft pink light and standing on a rumpled cloth of white linen. Again, I would dream that the leg was being unveiled; a cloth would fall and the leg would be shown. But the persons who removed the cloth with a pull of a cord were never ordinary people. Sometimes it would be a man without legs, standing there on two short stumps. A little man he was, in a little bowler hat and with the shortest of black striped trousers. He would stand there and pull the cord, to show the leg. Then would come the sound of clapping and then all would be blank again. Sometimes it was a woman who did the unveiling. She was particularly revolting. For instead of stumps she had arms, and stood on them, while her legs were at her shoulders. And yet her clothes seemed to fit. The first time I saw her in my dreams I thought that she just had extra long arms. Until she took off her gloves to pull the tasselled cord. And then I saw that it was with toes that she grasped the silk.

These were the first dreams I had about the leg. But frightening as they were there was one thing which I will always remember.

The leg was always *still*.

XIII

With the weeks the dreams began to change.

But the leg didn't go. The same old dreams. But different . . .

Always a long quiet street. A very ordinary street, sloping gently. It seemed to be a street on the edge of a small town. For the houses gave way at the end of the street to green fields and there was a little brook running across these fields and under the road. I could never see very plainly then, for in my dreams I always stood at one end of the street. Where the houses started, and well away from the green fields.

The houses were of new red brick and with small gardens in front, with wooden gates and stone steps up to the front door. There were gas lamps in that street and sometimes it was day, but more often night, when I stood at the end of that long quiet road.

Night-time and the lamps would be lit, soft pools of light with the steps of the houses in shadow. The row of lamps ending with the row of houses. Beyond, where the brook and the field lay, it was darkness.

But there was never light in any of the houses. Neither upstairs nor down. And the window panes stared darkly black, for the curtains were always gathered together in a little bundle at each side of the window, and never drawn.

And when in daytime my dreams took me to that street it was always winter. A grey cold day. For I never remember being in that street while the sun shone.

Day or night, no one ever came down the steps from the houses . . .

But day or night one thing always happened. Day or night it was always there.

The leg.

And day or night it was walking towards me as I stood at the end of the street. Daytime I could see it coming out of the mists at the end of the road, among the fields. Coming slowly along, and over the little bridge, through the hollow and up the road.

Nighttime, coming from out of the blackness into the yellow flickering light of the first gas lamp.

Ever up the street.

Ever up towards me.

It moved so easily, that leg. As if an invisible human were using it. All the joints working smoothly as it came along in certain steps.

Ever it would come towards me. But when the leg was a certain length of the street away from me, I would awake.

But with the nights that passed I knew one thing.

That each night the leg was a little nearer me before I awoke.

The distance was getting shorter. Between me and it.

It was coming ever nearer me as I stood there, waiting at the end of the lonely street.

XIV

Ever nearer me.

Until one night it was only the length of one lamp away from me . . .

Strangely for one week then I had no dreams. I was so relieved that I became kind again to Doreen. And she, to please me, would take off the leg before she went to bed.

For that week we were very happy.

But it was for one week only.

Then the dreams started again, quite suddenly.

The same street. The same houses. The same green fields in the distance. The same road dipping into the hollow.

And the leg.

But this time the dream was a little different.

It was *I* who was moving.

The leg stood poised in the centre of the road, just over the culvert which covered the brook.

And sometimes in the dream it was daylight. And at other times it was the night. In daytime I could plainly see the leg. But at night it was worse. I could not see it. But I knew it was standing there, beyond the light of the last gas lamp.

In each succeeding dream I moved nearer towards it. I had no longing to go. I wanted to run back or, if that could not be, to stay still. But on I had to go. And then the wish came. For every night in every dream I was moving nearer towards it. The fear behind my wish, the hope that I might reach the thing in the daytime of my dreams. For what if it should be darkness when I was driven on past the last glimmer from the last lamp? On, down the road and into the hollow, to where the brook ran. Every night I prayed that I should not dream. But I knew that that could not be. So I prayed that my dream should be of the light.

Doreen would watch me, praying by the side of the bed. Would watch my lips moving silent. She would look puzzled when I opened my eyes.

'You, Bill. You praying. Why, you never used to pray,' she'd say.

'Something came over me,' I'd say. And she would leave it at that.

But as I prayed I knew that she was watching me. Watching my moving lips and trying hard to follow what I was saying.

But the dreams of the light, and the dreams of the darkness came, and there was no succeeding order.

But daylight or darkness I moved ever up to the leg standing still in the centre of that dusty road, leading from the last houses of the town, into the country.

XV

But it was daylight when I reached it. That dream came on a November night. It was not far from Guy Fawkes day and that night the boys had been letting off fireworks in Welton. And Doreen had been nervous, jumping as the crackers went off. But about nine o'clock the noises stopped and then came the soft noise of the rain outside. A gentle wind blew up, too, at the corners of the streets. An odd night, and up in the bathroom I had looked through the two upper blank panes of glass above the frosted ones, before I switched on the light. Winter sky with black masses of clouds coming up from the west, rolling out the stars. As I bent to look out through the dark glass a sudden flurry of wind blew a spate of raindrops with a noisy clatter on the panes. Suddenly, I felt frightened. And jumped quickly to switch on the light. And all the time in the light bathroom, white with its chromium and tiles, I kept looking towards the darkness beyond those two blank panes of the window.

That night I was glad to get back to the light of the lounge and the murmur of the radio.

We went to bed early that night.

And with sleep it all came again . . .

XVI

The street was in daylight. The same sad street that always came to me.

The thing, too, was standing there. I could see it in the distance.

I was walking down the street. Rather fast. Faster than ever before.

And as I passed down the street, for the first time I saw people watching, a face behind a curtain, here and there. Just peeping at me as I moved along. But always drawing quickly back into the gloom of the rooms if I should happen to look their way.

As I passed the last house I could see the leg very plainly then. Plainer than ever before. It was balanced delicately there on its toe, the harness straps dangling at the one side.

The brook running under the road seemed to be swollen with muddy water, for it rushed with a roar through the culvert.

For the distance between the last house and the leg I was running. I knew that this time I was going to reach it. And when I reached it I knew what I was going to do. I was going to destroy it, destroy it for ever.

I reached it.

Slowly I put out my hand to touch it. As my hand touched it I felt suddenly glad, and with savage glee I pushed it. The leg swayed on its toe, it seemed to be so delicately balanced. I pushed it harder and it fell on the gritty, grey surface of the road.

I caught hold of it by the pointed toe and raised it high above my head like an axe. Then brought it crashing down on the hard road.

It broke at the knee. The thigh part I took and held by the straps, banging it hard down on the brick parapet of the culvert. The metal slowly dented and flattened. Then I threw it far up into the muddy water of the flooded brook. It fell with a splash and the water splashed out over the green grass of the meadow.

The calf portion I broke off the foot by hitting again on the road. Then I flattened it by stamping on it. After that I threw it away down the stream away from and opposite to the thigh portion.

The foot I heaved into a small clump of rushes at the bottom of the bridge.

I looked around me. There was nothing left, nothing.

My foe was ended.

I went back the way I had come, up the slope and to where the houses started. I was walking gaily in the certain knowledge that it had been destroyed and would trouble me no more.

Halfway along the street I noticed that the people were still there behind the curtain, peeping out. But more bold this time.

They were not looking at me. But rather past me, down the street, the way I had come. One old man with white hair and quiet grey eyes was further out from the curtains than the others. He was sitting on the windowsill. He, too, was looking down the street to the open country.

And as I passed his window he knocked twice, hard on the glass. I looked at him. He just pointed with a lean brown finger to the way I had come. Then he darted back into the darkness of the room.

As he pointed I knew, and I looked over my shoulder.

The thing was following me, gracefully and quickly along on its toe . . .

XVII

I knew then that it had beaten me. And with that knowledge came the realisation. The realisation that in one way
only could I destroy the leg which haunted me. In one way
only. By destroying she who loved it and gave it being.

The determination came that I must destroy Doreen.
How?

XVIII

Many were the ways I thought of. And many were the plans I laid. But they were all faulty in as much as I would be discovered. And it was part of my plan that I should – must – have many years of happiness. Free from the thing which had given me so much pain.

How then should Doreen go?

My final plans were wonderful.

I could not be caught.

For Doreen would help to kill herself.

XIX

The morning after that last dream I stayed in bed till about ten o'clock as I had no appointments that day. I had intended to spend a day on mechanic work, the making of dentures and plates.

A short while later Doreen brought my breakfast up to me. I knew that it would be coming for below our room was the kitchen. I could hear the clink of dishes and the loud shrill whistle of the kettle, and the dry smell of toast-making filling the house. Suddenly I felt that she was very dear to me. This making of my breakfast to bring to me in bed, for she knew that I was worn out with my night-mares, as she called them.

The whistle of the kettle ceased and I knew that she was making the coffee. A regular series of clinks came and I could see her laying out the white clean crocks on the breakfast tray. The harsh roar of the newly lit fire.

And then I could hear her opening the kitchen door and the way she pulled it with the inside of her finger.

Now she would be climbing the stairs . . .

Then all changed. For it was no ordinary step I could hear. No regular even ascent. But a step and a pause, and

54

then a louder harder rap. I could imagine her climbing up. Her sound whole lovely leg first. And then she would pause a moment to draw the other thing up. And so it went on as she climbed up. Longer it took, much longer, to climb the stairs than it would have taken an ordinary woman.

How could she balance the tray, the tray for me, through it all?

I lay back in our bed hating her. Hating her for having to climb the stairs with my breakfast. Hating her for having to remind me that she existed, was in being. That she was different. For while she lived, it too lived. And while it lived there could be no peace for me.

The same uneven walk up to the bedroom door. And then she called out, 'I've brought your breakfast darling.'

I called out thank you and leant out from the bed to open the door for her.

She laid the tray on the bed. It was a little time before I could look up and say, 'Thank you, Doreen.'

And then looking into her face I saw that she was ill. And illness of a nature not new to my professional eye.

For her face was swollen on the one side. Swollen and very red.

'Doreen,' I said. 'Your face.'

'Yes, darling,' she replied. 'Yes, I must have an abscess or something. It's terribly painful and the gum is swollen and tender inside. It throbs like hell, darling. Do wish you'd have a look at it and do something for it. But eat your breakfast first.'

She sat on the edge of the bed while I ate the meal she had brought. Sat there while I tried hard not to look at her legs. For the one was stiff and straight on the bedside rug. How I hated her that morning for not wearing stockings.

It was while I was eating my breakfast that my plan formed. It was a clever plan that came to my mind as I sat there, watching her one white hand smoothing the swollen redness of her jaw.

Putting on a dressing gown I went down with her to the surgery.

There I set the water running in the unit and switched on the lights. Laid a white napkin over her throat, for I always treated her just like any other patient.

It was a back lower molar which was the trouble. The crown had recently broken but the trouble must have started some time ago, for the pulp canal was gangrenous and decayed. The gum itself was very much inflamed too.

'It's a very bad tooth, Doreen. I never guessed that it was quite so bad. I must put a dressing on it now to ease the pain and then we can see what we can do with it when the inflammation has died down a little.'

'Thank you, darling. It's been aching all night. But I didn't want to wake you. You were sleeping, but tossing so.'

'Those nightmares, Doreen. You know what I go through.'

'Poor Bill, I know.'

As if she knew . . .

I put on a dressing and painted the gum with a local anaesthetic to ease the pain. I could see the pain go from her face as I painted on the solution.

'Thank you, darling, that's wonderful.'

'Good, Doreen. Now, I think that we can save that tooth.'

'Save it? But I thought the only remedy for a tooth with a decayed pulp canal was extraction?'

'Not always,' I told her. 'Not always. This is a new treatment which has been tried with the sulpha drugs. Listen and I will explain to you.'

She sat there in the chair while I found a recent copy of one of my professional journals which I had filed away. I found the article. And then I explained to her how I was going to save the tooth. 'You are my wife now, not my patient. That's why I'm going to explain it all to you, Doreen.'

She laughed, then settled back in the chair as I explained the treatment to her.

'You know, darling, that in the past it has always been necessary to take out such teeth which are abscessed and which have a gangrenous pulp canal like the one that's troubling you, Doreen. Well, now it seems that there's a new treatment which clears up the trouble and sometimes enables the tooth to be built up again. It is necessary first to clean out the pulp canal with a special needle and then to flush with peroxide of hundred-volumes strength. As you know, darling, the ordinary peroxide is either ten- or twenty-volumes strength. So you can see that this is very much stronger and will hence have a very powerful cleansing action. With the peroxide and alternately to it, we will use another powerful cleansing agent, sodium hypochlorite. These solutions are flooded into the tooth until the gangrenous matter has been cleared away and the pulp canal is clean.

'Now the cavity is flooded with sterile, distilled water. And now comes the important part of the treatment. One of the series of drugs you've heard me talking about is the sulpha range, darling. These may be sulphathiazole, or sulphapyridine, or sulphadiazine. In this case I shall use sulphathiazole. This I will introduce into the flooded cavity until the solution becomes saturated. Then I shall put on a dressing and leave it for a week or so. Then it may be necessary by that time to repeat the treatment. Then I hope that all the pus from the abscess sac will have gone and that the tooth socket will be healthy.

'On this healthy base I hope to build up a new tooth for you, my darling.'

She said thank you for all your trouble. And I told her that it was no trouble at all and that it was a pleasure to do anything for her. But I told her, too, that I couldn't start on the treatment right away. That I would have to go into the city to fetch some of the drug. I asked her had the pain gone from her face now?

She nodded and smiled awkwardly, for her face was still very swollen. Then she got up from the chair, swaying to get her balance and putting out her hands to my shoulder to balance herself. And her last words before she left for the kitchen were that she was so glad that her husband was a dentist.

XX

After tea that day much of the ache had gone from Doreen's face. And with the evening the sun shone strongly over the High Street of Welton and there was a soft warm wind blowing down from the Welsh hills. So I suggested to Doreen that we did a little gardening. But let me say that our gardening was not of the usual sort, digging in quarter of an acre of soft ground or among neatly set flower beds. Our gardening was very much of the at home sort. We tended the small window boxes which made our home look so different from the others in the High Street of Welton. The window boxes painted green and which summer or winter we always kept tidy, and full of gay flowers or with dangling creepers. They were our especial joy, those window boxes.

So when I said gardening, Doreen gladly agreed. I knew she would.

For all this was part of my plan.

Doreen took the window box in the room over the surgery. I stood behind her as she raked over the rich earth and as she poured a little water around the roots of the green geraniums. Down below in the High Street all was quiet. The first-house pictures had started about half an hour ago. And so all would be still in the street until the second house started in the only cinema in the town.

Doreen was very busy raking and prodding the earth.

I waited. Waited until she was working to the right of the box.

I waited until her hand was just by the nail. A nail which had not been put in straight when the box had been made. A nail now rusty with the weather and the damp soil. Still quite sharp and clearly seen in the one corner of the box.

I stumbled. Quite sharply, I fell against her. Hitting her elbow.

It happened as I planned.

The nail grazed her finger so that she gave a sharp little breath.

'Darling, I'm so, so sorry,' I said. 'So terribly sorry.'

I put my arm around her and led her back into the room and sat her on a chair.

It was only a small scratch and hardly any blood showed. I put a piece of sticking plaster on it and after I had said sorry again, we went back to our gardening.

Until we had to give it up. For the bending over the window box always made the stump of her leg ache so.

XXI

That night I did not dream.

I almost abandoned my plan. But I knew that if I did that the dream would soon come back again. And maybe I would never have such a chance again to end it all.

The next morning I rang up the two clients who had made appointments. I rang them up and told them to cancel their engagements. I asked them to come again on the same day next week.

After that I told Doreen that I would have to go to the city in the Midlands to buy the sulphathiazole to pack into her tooth.

She wondered a little at that and asked was it not possible to buy some at the chemist's in Welton?

I told her, no. Impossible. I must have the sterile preparation. And they would certainly have none of that in the chemist's shop in Welton.

I asked her would she like to come with me?

She said she would.

And so we went down to the station and caught the connection for the morning express into the Midland city.

Getting in and out of railway carriages was always difficult for Doreen. But people were always wonderfully kind
and helpful. They always looked so sorry for her. The men
would glance at her one shapely leg, then at the other leg,
after that at her face, and then purse their lips a little.
Women, usually so very cruel to another attractive woman,
were quite kind to Doreen. They'd whisper, but always so
that she could hear. Poor dear. What a shame.

Arrived at the city I left Doreen in a café and told her
that I would shortly be back.

And now came some of the very important parts of my
plan.

Firstly I had to buy the sulphathiazole powder.

To buy this I went to the warehouse of a dental supply
company where I was known. The powder they had in
stock, ready sterilised, in 5 G quantities. Would that be
sufficient? Yes, yes, quite sufficient and I explained to them
for what purpose I wanted the drug. They were very interested and said that only the day before they had supplied
some sulphathiazole to another dentist for the very same
purpose. They hoped that the treatment would be success-
ful. Would I sign the poisons register? The drug was a
Schedule 4 poison, they explained. Willingly, oh so willingly
I signed that book giving my name, my professional qualifi-
cation, my address, the amount of the drug, and the use for
which I wanted it. For all this would help my plan . . .

I left the offices of the company and made my way to
purchase the second item necessary for my plan.

It was to the offices of a large firm of manufacturing
chemists from whom I had had one or two items of drugs,

but always by post, mainly injections and other similar items.

The clerk in the sales department was very obliging when I told her that I wanted six phials of tetanus toxoid. She asked me was I a professional man? I told her I was. Then she asked me again, it's the tetanus *toxoid* you want, sir, not the antitoxin. The toxoid, I said again. The toxoid, please, six ampoules.

She went away to the refrigerator to get them. For all such preparations are best stored at an even cool temperature, although they will keep their potency at room temperature for some time.

This tetanus toxoid! Let me explain.

It is used in small doses to produce an active immunity against tetanus in the individual. A small amount injected produces a small attack of tetanus. His body brings its defensive mechanism into play and for some time afterwards the individual is immune to tetanus infection.

But in *small* doses only is the toxoid used to produce a *mild* attack of tetanus.

In larger doses . . .

Thus you will see that the toxoid is potentially a dangerous substance. That in small amounts it is beneficial in that it will produce a small attack of tetanus which is resisted in the body by the production of antibodies. These will give the person injected with the toxoid an active acquired immunity against any tetanus infection in the future.

But note that I said in *small* quantities.

But what, what if more than the prescribed quantity of the toxoid is introduced into the body? What if the system is flooded? If the defensive mechanism is flooded before the antibodies can be produced? Then the person will have a tetanus infection. He or she will in fact be injected with the very disease itself, if more than the maximum dose of the toxoid is injected into the system.

The person will, therefore, die.

On this was based my plan.

My plan to rid myself of the leg.

The only solution for me, the only freedom I could get lay in destroying Doreen.

The way I was going to kill Doreen was wonderfully, wonderfully clever.

It was so clever that they never found out. And but for what I choose to write no one would have known.

If I had not written no one in Welton, no one in England itself would have guessed the real reason why my wife, Doreen, died. They could have proved nothing against me. Nothing.

My plan then, was this. The plan which I followed. Which worked, perfectly.

And which should have given me freedom.

XXII

I was going to murder Doreen. But it would seem no murder. For she would die of tetanus infection. But I would have introduced that infection.

You will recall that Doreen had scratched her hand while we were gardening with the window boxes. I had been the cause of that wound for I had lurched against her. Now the tetanus bacillus is known to be plentiful in the soil. So to the outside world it would seem that Doreen had caught the infection that evening when we were gardening. That was my protection. For no one could prove that she had *not* caught the infection then. But I would not have introduced the sulphathiazole I had bought into her tooth. I would introduce the tetanus toxoid. I would pump in not one, which would be an excessive dose in itself, but the contents of the six phials.

That would give her sufficient massive infection to cause her to quickly die.

That was my plan.

XXIII

The dose of the tetanus toxoid was 1 cc per week for two weeks.

Each of the phials contained 50 cc. Fifty doses. And I was going to inject the toxoid from my stock of six phials until finally Doreen died.

We travelled back that day from the city. It was evening when we arrived, back in Welton. A cold wet dismal evening with the wind blowing wet against our legs as we walked up from the station. I could feel my knees damp through the flannel of my trousers. And Doreen stumped along by my side lifting her leg with the rolling gait she had developed, and which is the only way that a person with an artificial leg from the thigh can walk. The muscles of the back come into action to lift the leg from the ground and swing it along.

We reached the house, cold and quiet with the fires out and only the cold water in the taps. The dead grey ashes on the hearth and unwashed breakfast things in a dirty heap in the sink. The one water tap half on and a little trickle of water had been running all day, washing the grease on the top plate, down to the white china. The open packet of cornflakes on the table, the greased paper lining folded over, ready to seal the packet for putting away.

I lit the gas under a kettle and went through back into the hall. Doreen had hung up her plastic raincoat. The rain had gathered into little drops on the slippery surface and was dropping into quick streams on the red tiles of the hall floor.

The pool of water wet on the small fancy tiles there under her coat, the fabric of mine, dark and stained with the rain.

I stood watching her. She raised her artificial leg stiffly on to the second step of the stair. And with a further effort on to the third. On the second stair, staining the deep pile, the mark of her heel showed wet and deep.

Her leg out straight now. She moved her sound leg back a little on the floor of the hall to get her balance.

Leaning on the door of the kitchen I watched her.

Always this after being out in the rain.

The stocking on the one leg wet and clinging to the metal. She raised her skirt up and unsuspended the stocking and peeled it down the grey metal.

'Very wet,' she said, and I nodded back, saying that it was raining heavy.

She rolled the stocking down to the ankle, leaving the metal wet and moist.

Then swaying slightly to keep her balance she took off her shoe. And then the stocking.

Then put her fingers into the toe of the stocking and spread them out, looking through them. 'Standing the strain well, darling,' she said.

'Good pair those, Doreen,' I said.

She held the inside of the toe with her hand and turned the stocking inside out.

'Must dry it,' she said.

'You must, Doreen.'

And then followed what I knew would.

Always this after being out in the rain.

She lifted up her skirt again and unbuckled the straps which held the leg.

As she lifted it off I gave her my shoulder for her to lean on.

With the leg in her hand she shook it. The soft plop and splash of water inside.

Her head on one side she listened to the sound.

'Must have been raining heavy, darling, there's more than usual.'

'Heavy rain,' I said. 'Heavy rain and the wind.'

Then holding the leg in her one hand and the stocking in the other she hopped away.

Hopped away and I following. To the sink in the kitchen.

And there, leaning against the draining board she turned the leg upside down and poured away the water which had gathered inside.

XXIV

It was after supper that the pain came back to Doreen's tooth. Quite suddenly she gripped the edge of the table firmly in her hands. I could see her mouth set hard and the look of fear in the way her eyelids wrinkled together.

After a moment she spoke. 'It's come back,' she said. 'The pain to my tooth.'

'Bad?' I asked her. 'Bad?'

'Very,' she answered, with her hand cupped to her lower jaw.

Then I decided to start my operation sooner than I had at first planned. Do it in the morning had been my scheme. But the pain starting now would be a good excuse for me to start at once.

It was ten o'clock.

From the house next door the music from the radio came faintly through the wall. The sound of a high-pitched man's voice singing to the music. That son from the house next door, always singing or whistling. When the house was still we heard him so.

'He's at it again,' I said. She nodded and started to sway her head, then her shoulders and her body swayed too.

'The pain, darling. It's so bad.'

'Would you like me to do the little job now, Doreen?'

'Isn't it too late? And aren't you too tired?'

'Anything to stop your pain,' I told her. 'Anything. You've had your fair share of pain in this life already. Let me do it now, to stop the ache.'

'Do it now, darling. Do it now.'

We went through to the surgery, first putting on the coffee percolator ready for when it would all be over. She wanted to do that. And I let her. For what use to tell her . . .

The way she walked, hopping from one piece of furniture to the next. From the arm of a chair to the corner of the sideboard. I could see the bulge on her thigh as the loose stump bumped against the quilted housecoat she was wearing. I couldn't stand that, the sight of that lovely padded material thrusting out under the pressure of the stump.

I sent her back to put on her leg. It must be with her in the defeat. I told her that it would be very awkward for her in the chair with one leg only. She hopped out and I waited until she came back with the other leg strapped on. She was tired, I could see that in the way she slowly swung her leg. The walking and the train journey, the hopping – that always tired her – and the pain from her tooth. The blue lines of gooseflesh under her red eyes showing very plain against the redness of her one cheek and the paleness of the other.

A sudden feeling of pity and tenderness came to me and I gently helped her into the chair and eased her down into the leather seat.

'I get tired so easily now, Bill.'

I went out to the hall and to my raincoat and got out the tetanus toxoid and the sulphathiazole.

I took them to the surgery.

'Draw the curtains, Bill,' she said to me. 'Draw the curtains, we don't want people to see in.'

No, we didn't want people to see in.

I drew across the heavy green curtains. Carried the toxoid and the sulphathiazole and laid them on the little glass shelf at the back of the chair. The shelf so tactfully placed.

'What a lot of bottles, darling. You're not going to inject all those into me are you?'

'Just some local anaesthetics I've brought along with me for future use.'

She turned around in the chair to watch me as I took out a 10 cc syringe from the cupboard and laid it by the bottles. And by the bottles I laid a small 2 cc dental syringe. The tetanus toxoid I had carefully placed with its label away from her.

'Two syringes? Why two, Bill?'

Damn her and her questions. Why did she have to ask so many?

Ask no questions, I told her. You're my patient now, not my wife.

She wriggled frontwards again, her hands folded in her lap.

From the street beyond the green curtains came the soft patter of the rain on the pavement. The splash of a passing car, and sometimes a few drops of rain blown against the window pane.

'It's still raining,' she said.
Still raining, I answered back.

I got out the peroxide and the sodium hypochlorite solution. The needles ready to clean out the pulp cavity.

I folded a serviette about her neck. Switched on the
electric globes over her chair . . .

XXV

Outside the noise of the rain was becoming fainter. But a wind was rising and shaking the old sash windows, the green curtains swaying out a little.

And then I started work.

I injected first a local anaesthetic into her gum.

Then I started methodically to clean out the pulp canal of the infected tooth. I flushed out the cavity with peroxide of 100-volumes strength, drying it out with paper points, and then flushing in the sodium hypochlorite solution.

Several times I carried this out, until the pulp canal was fairly clean.

Doreen lay back in the chair, her hands still folded and her eyes closed. Breathing short and fast and with a little groan in the outward breath sometimes.

I handed her a glass of mouthwash and she spat out into the bowl.

'Only the sulphathiazole now, Doreen,' I said.

She leaned back again and I took up a syringe and made a percentage solution of the sulphathiazole. I filled the 2 cc syringe and very carefully laid the syringe aside.

I took up the other syringe, the larger one. Then I opened a phial of the tetanus toxoid. Read the label twice: *Contents 50 cc. Dose 1 cc twice a week.*

Ay, 1 cc twice a week.

I filled the 10 cc syringe, pushing the needle through the rubber cap and inverting the bottle to draw off the contents. Then with the syringe held very carefully in my hand I asked Doreen to lie far back. And I carefully placed the needle deep, very deep into the cavity of the tooth. I started to press home the plunger. She winced a little as the needle sank down and again as I withdrew the needle, the syringe now empty.

'Gosh, that was far down, darling. Was it necessary to go quite so far down?'

'Very necessary,' I told her. And told her that there was more to come.

I was warming to the job now. She was infected now, on the way to death.

'More?' she asked.

I think she must have guessed that there was something queer because she then asked me why I looked so odd and went on to say that I was hurting her terribly with that needle which I was pushing so very deep down into her gum.

And so then I had to be very kind and talk to her soothingly. I did not want her to become frightened and run away.

'It's all right, my darling,' I said. 'I'll give you another shot of local so that I won't hurt you next time.'

So I gave her some local anaesthetic again and then I filled the 10 cc syringe once more and gave the whole of it this time.

And again, again, again. Many times.

Until she became too dazed to ask why were there so many and to ask which was the last.

The symptoms started to appear.

Yes, the symptoms of tetanus on my wife, Doreen, as she lay there in my dental chair in our front room, my surgery. As she lay there that cold wet evening, with the wind howling around the house. The wind blowing and few walking the streets of Welton. And those that passed my front window knew nothing of what was going on behind the cosy lighted greenness. Knew nothing. And soon the streets would be empty. It would be late. But it did not matter. I had the whole night in which to kill her.

Death in tetanus poisoning is due to a toxin which is produced by the bacteria in the infected area. This finds its way to the spinal cord and makes the central nervous system very, very sensitive indeed.

One of the first symptoms of infection is a stiffness around the source of the infection; this later spreads and always results in a locking of the jaws. Doreen's site of infection was the jaw, hence the locking came fairly soon that night. Always too comes action and reaction in the muscles around the jaws with spasms and the features drawn and pulled. Her teeth came fully into view as her lips curled back and she seemed to have the usual sardonic grin so typical of the facial features once the fatal stages of tetanus have set in. After a time this locked nature of her muscles went to those of her back, her chest and her arms and the one sound leg she had. Her whole body at first bent rigid backwards, but before long it set leaning over to the side of her missing leg. But she was not locked hard in this position, there were reflexes and the typical 'frequently recurring convulsive seizures'. How right the medical textbooks are when they say 'in such attacks there is great suffering and the face is indication of agony'.

Soon she started to sweat . . . and that was the worst of all, to see her there with the perspiration pouring down her twisting agonised face.

Her mind was quite clear at moments in between the spasms. Then she wanted to get up.

And I had to hold her down. But even when her mind was clear she could not speak. Only strange strangled noises came through the locked jaws.

Death, they say, usually comes from the respiratory muscles being too rigid to function. Or it may come from fatigue due to loss of sleep.

But she lived through the night and until the next morning.

By then she was nearly dead.

With the dawn the wind that had been blowing all the night went away. With the coming of the light I left her. It was certain then that she would die. She lay there convulsed and twitching, the artificial leg oddly twisted and out of line with the rest of her.

I went through to the kitchen to the coffee which she had put on before she had left the kitchen for the last time. The water had boiled dry.

But I needed coffee. I was tired that morning. Tired with holding her down and the lack of sleep. I lit the gas and put a kettle on to boil. Took out the bottle of liquid coffee essence, new and unopened. She'd bought it only the day before from the counter store in the city. Will do me good when I want a quick cup for a headache she'd said.

I took out cups and saucers and tried to unscrew the top of the bottle. But the metal top was jammed and it wouldn't unscrew. I held it in a corner of a tea towel and tried to grip it that way but the thing kept slipping. I tried too, heating the metal to loosen it, but it would not loosen. So finally I got out the tin opener and made a hole in the top with the pointed end of the tool. Tried to pour out the coffee. But it wouldn't run, and as I was watching it, held upside down, I noticed quite suddenly that my hands were shaking.

I, a dentist with my hands trembling. After trying to open a bottle of coffee essence.

But I told myself that it was the worry and the lack of sleep. The worry and the lack of sleep.

Then I tried to knock off the neck of the bottle against the edge of the gas stove. But as I did that the glass splintered and I was afraid that there might be some powdered glass in the liquid. For my old fear of things was coming back. And as I looked at my trembling hands I knew that it would be hard to carry on with my profession.

Tea it would have to be after all my efforts to have coffee. And I wanted the coffee so very much.

It was as I was about to pour out the tea that I noticed it. Noticed that I had laid two cups, two saucers on the table. It would be hard not to slip on these things.

I put away the one cup and the one saucer. Put them away in the cupboard. The rows of the china which was

78

our everyday set. The best away in the china cupboard with the glass doors. The list pinned to the inside of the cupboard door. List of all the contents of the cupboard pinned there in the early days of our married life.

And somehow as I drank the tea, alone there in the kitchen, that morning I had the fear, the terrible fear that perhaps I would miss her.

But by now it would be all over.

And there was no going back, now.

XXVI

I went back to the surgery.

By now she was dead.

Others would think that she now looked rather terrible. For the death was not a pleasant one.

But I who had watched her through the night was glad that it was all over. For now at least she was *still* and her body stayed in one terrifying twist. It was not now forever moving.

One or two important things yet I had to do before I called the others in.

First to get rid of the toxoid.

I took the empty phials up to the bathroom. One or two had a few ccs. of liquid still in them. I emptied these down the lavatory and pulled the chain.

The empty phials and cartons I took down to the kitchen. And there I burnt the cartons, stirring the ashes to make certain that they had all burnt away. To make finally sure I lit the gas poker under the black charred ashes and let it burn away for a few minutes.

The small bottles I soaked in water until the labels came away. The six wet labels! I was careful to count them! I held them before the fire until they were dry. And then I burnt them directly on top of the gas poker. The empty bottles I took to the surgery. Three I filled with hydrogen peroxide solution, the other three I filled with sodium hypochlorite solution, writing neat labels for them all. I put the six bottles in a straight row on the glass shelf at the back of her body.

I took the 2 cc syringe which contained the unused sulphathiazole solution up to the bathroom. Exactly half the solution I squirted down the washbasin and let the cold tap run on it for a time. The half-empty 2 cc syringe I took back to the surgery and laid on the glass shelf.

The large syringe which I had used to inject the toxoid I took to the kitchen and swilled it in hot water and then carefully dried it. Took it back to the surgery and filled it with some of the peroxide from one of the small bottles which I had filled.

One final check . . .

And now all was ready to call the others in.

XXVII

Now to call the others in.

Important this.

And I was afraid that here I might fail.

I knew that if I waited too long and thought too much that I would fail.

So I quickly went to shave.

I put the kettle on to boil.

And then I went through to look at her once again.

I stood watching her until the whistle of the kettle came shrill from the kitchen. I went out from the surgery, closing the door gently behind me.

In the hall the rattle of the letterbox as the postman pushed the letters through. They fell with a flop on the tiles of the hall. Then all still again.

I picked up the letters. Bills. One from the hairdresser for having her hair done.

Back in the kitchen I poured out the water into my shaving mug and decided to shave straight away.

Upstairs and looking at my face in the round mirror on the wall above the bath, I seemed to see a change there already. Not the change which should be. Not the freedom. The freedom from the thing that was haunting me, that I hoped had gone with her. But a new fear seemed to be there in my face. Plain to see. It's nothing I told myself. Just lack of sleep that's all. That and the concentration needed to put her out. Anybody would be like that after a night awake watching his wife die.

But why could I not keep my eyes fixed on the mirror? Why not, as I shaved? Why was I looking right and left. And often behind. Very often behind. I washed the lather off my face before I had finished shaving. Washed the lather off my face with the little square of face flannel hanging dry on the tap of the bath. The little face flannel with the faintly embroidered edge and smelling faintly of her. The sweet-smelling powder that she had washed off her face some night gone by.

Strange how the fragrance lingered.

You should wash out the flannel – and as I said it I had turned. Because I could have sworn that she was standing there and that I was talking to her. And for the moment I had forgotten . . .

Ass I said. Ass that you are. Talking to yourself.

Footsteps to the back door below. The dull clink of the full milk bottles as they were laid on the doorstep. Then the lighter clink as the empties were taken away, swaying by the neck in the milkman's hand.

I went down and took in the milk. Long time since I had done this. Wonder how she bent each morning to get them in?

An hour to go before I could go out and fetch them in. One hour.

I thought that it would have been less.

An hour.

How should I pass it?

How?

A bath. That would do it. A bath to wash away the tiredness from my body.

Upstairs in the bathroom I turned on the hot tap waiting for the steam to rise. But the kitchen fire had been out, out all night. The water was only lukewarm.

I went down again to the kitchen to light the gas heater. But the gas had run out. A shilling for the slot.

Wonder where she kept the little pile of shillings. She always stored them, somewhere.

It took me a long time to find them. Piled high at the back of the china cupboard, behind the teapot with the half-broken spout.

She had been like that. Forever keeping old half-broken china. Had always said that it would come in useful someday.

The shilling in the slot. The wait for the water to boil.

And then in the bathroom for the first time in many years I bolted the door behind me. Even testing the door to see that the bolt held firm. And when in the bath I closed my eyes to wash my face, I could see her, very, very clear . . .

XXVIII

The run to the police station: the fetching of the doctor: the story at the coroner's inquest.

It all worked, perfectly.

The next night I slept.

The verdict at the inquest was *Accidental death*.

My plan had worked.

I was free.

We buried her in the local churchyard, and hundreds came to the funeral.

It was when I got back to the house that I found it . . .

God, how I cursed those fools of undertakers. Those idiots. Why had I been content to have the job done by the local firm? Why had I not got a city firm who knew their job instead of these fools who were builders and joiners and heaven knows what.

For the funeral it had been necessary to carry the coffin from the hospital mortuary to the house. They had done that the morning of the funeral. They had laid it in the upstairs bedroom to wait until the burial in the afternoon. And up there they must have unscrewed the coffin ready for me to see her, but I had refused to look and had not gone up to the room.

Oh, the idiots, the asses. For they had taken the leg out of the coffin and left it behind. Propped it up so very carefully in the corner of the bedroom.

XXIX

There it was, neatly standing in the corner of the bedroom. And my very first thought was how out of place it seemed there against the gay floral wallpaper.

Why had they to leave it here? Why could they not at least have asked me about it? Why could they not have put it in the coffin with her?

For I had done murder to get rid of it and its mistress. And I thought that they would have taken it too away from me. For I feared that thing. As long as its material side was about my house I feared too the unseen power which the thing had to haunt and hinder me. To make my life hell.

The local undertakers. I would ring them up and ask them why they had done this to me.

I dialled the number from the phone in the hall. With the steady burr of the phone in my ear I waited.

That fabric mac of hers just by my hand, the smell of it filling the hall.

I would have to sell her clothes now.

The voice asking me . . .

Why did you have to leave the leg in my bedroom? Why did you not bury it with the body.

A little pause. A little cough. Odd my question I suppose. So callous.

Another voice now.

The principal.

I asked again, why did you not bury the leg with Mrs Sterrill? Why not?

So that was the reason. Such things are valuable. Maybe you would want to sell the leg, or something.

Or something . . .

Thank you, I said, Would you care to buy?

They said no.

Breathing heavy they rang off rather quickly.

Ah well, the thing would be fairly harmless I suppose. What with its mistress dead; and she was the power behind the thing; with her dead, it too, would be dead.

But just in case, in case it still had power, I must send the thing away. Anywhere, to anywhere. But it must not spend the night with me under the same roof.

Back in the kitchen came the thought.

Revenge.

It had been very attached to its mistress. Maybe it would want to avenge her death. That was my fear.

It had been vicious before, that leg. God knows what it would be like with revenge in its soul.

Soul? Why must we assume that there is a God part in every soul? Why not Satan have his little hold, his little plot too?

I must send it right away to the makers, the leg must go this afternoon. They would be glad to have it.

I went out and up the street to the greengrocers. The tubs of fruit outside and the mixed strong smell of the flowers and vegetables inside, all as it had always been, familiar and friendly.

Little Mr Jones himself came to attend to me, wiping his hands on the corner of his blue apron.

He said hullo to me and told me how sad he was to hear of my loss. Sad, sad loss, such a lovely woman was your wife. Always a joy to serve her.

I told him I wanted a box, so by so. I showed him with hands the size of the box I would want to pack a leg in.

He had a box. Just the right size. One that he had a new scales in.

He wanted to send it around for me. The boy won't be a jiffy.

But I said that I'd take it myself. I dare not leave it. For supposing the boy forgot to bring it?

And the leg must go off tonight.

XXX

The late afternoon I spent in packing the leg.

The case which I had from the shop was ideal. It was long and narrow but quite deep and it had inside it all the packing material which had been used to pack the scales.

There was still the sweet delicate perfume of her on that thing of metal. The perfume from the talcum powder which she used to dust the leather straps. The chafing and rubbing had at first rawed her skin; until she had the idea of dusting the leather bands to take away some of the soreness.

And although after a time her skin had hardened and calloused, still she had kept up the habit of dusting the upper part of the limb each day with the finest talcum powder.

The smell was still there. And as I raised the leg to put it on the table the perfume seemed to rise in a slow steady stream and cling in my nostrils so that she herself seemed to be in the room. And after the first startling feeling of her nearness had passed away came a slight feeling of sickness. And after that had gone there remained the same empty depressed feeling of fear centred in my groins and arching together over the pit of my stomach.

I wrapped the leg first in many layers of corrugated paper. Many, many layers, swathing the metal around and around. For the limb must be in good condition when it reached the makers. For if it was damaged they might return it.

And then I would have the thing on my hands again.

Then I laid it in the box and carefully pressed around it all the shavings and the sawdust that had been in the box before. I nailed on the lid, the blows of the hammer making the china in the kitchen cupboard jump and rattle.

I fastened on a label and made to write the address of the makers. But I could not remember it. I had to go upstairs and to the small bureau in our bedroom where she had kept all her personal things.

As I lifted the lid of the small desk and let it fall open the same smell was there. For in the one corner of the desk was the tin of talcum powder.

It took me long to find the bill. Turning over the papers it was odd the strange little things that she had kept. All of which I suppose had some meaning to her. Little cuttings from the local press about the wedding of some man – an old boyfriend perhaps. An invitation here and there. Bills for the oddest things.

At last I found it. The receipt for the leg.

I took it downstairs and there carefully copied the address from the billhead on to the label on the box.

Then I took the box out and down to the station, my two arms around it and clinging to it. For it was heavy and twice I had to set it down on end while I gained my breath.

At the station I left it ready to go on the next passenger train, back to the suppliers in the Midlands.

And as I walked up the street from the station I began to notice the things in the streets again. It was long since I had looked at the signs outside the local offices of the insurance company. How some of the street lamps had been painted. The new island they had put to slow up the traffic by the station.

Walking up the street I noticed as never before the little things. How the nuns hurried like black beetles from the convent to the church over the road, crossing the street quickly from one gas-lighted pavement to the other.

And how the wind tore the adverts pasted to the walls, and flapped the loose pieces savagely from the weathered wood.

Soon the leg would be on the train.

Away and out of my life.

On entering the house I felt almost gay.

I switched on the radio and cooked myself a meal. Tonight I would sleep. I was quite sure of that. I knew it.

For she was gone. And in my wallet was the receipt for the cash that I had paid for the fare of the leg.

After the meal I took out that small buff-coloured slip:

For conveyance of one wooden box per passenger train.

My protection. Proof that it had gone.

And yet?

I rang up the station.

My box. Had it gone?

Yes, yes. Just gone they said. Did I want to withhold it? They could do that if . . .

Good God. No.

I just wanted to make sure it had gone, that's all.

Goodbye.

Goodbye.

I just wanted to make sure.

That evening I read the daily papers for the last few days.

Listened to the radio.

And that high-pitched singing from the house next door. I could whistle now to accompany it.

But I would take no chances I told myself. No chances at all.

Wouldn't sleep in that room.

Wouldn't give myself a chance to be disturbed there.

That double bed, and the smell there of that talcum powder. All her clothes up there and her silky undies.

Oh no. Too many memories up there. Be a temptation to the devil himself if I was to sleep there.

The leg was the dearest thing on earth to her. And now it was gone. But she'd been fond of her dresses too. Part of her maybe would be in the train with the leg. But perhaps a part of her would still be here in the bedroom?

So not to give her the slightest chance of disturbing me tonight, I'd sleep down in the kitchen. I'd bring the divan bed down from the guest room. It would fit nicely before the fire. Comfortable too.

But then she'd spent so much time in her kitchen that maybe she'd come back there?

Christ man. Pull yourself together. You're not afraid of *her* if she does come. As long as the leg is away you have nothing to fear.

Down there in the kitchen the people next door seemed to be so near.

Just open the back door and there just over the two-foot wall was their back door.

Just open the door and over the wall and you're there.

I started to carry the divan bed downstairs rolling the mattress in front of me. But it caught on the banisters and I had to push at it very hard with my feet. Then it rolled suddenly to the bottom of the stairs and crashed into the hall stand.

Then I rolled it through into the kitchen.

Nice spring mattress this. I wouldn't bother to get the rest of the bed down. This mattress would do fine.

This and a few bedclothes.

I went through into our bedroom to fetch my pyjamas.

Couldn't find the pair I had worn when we had last slept together. Probably they'd be in the airing cupboard.

They were. All on top of a heap of her things. Soft and warm as I put my hand to draw them out. I sorted out my pyjamas from her things and wondered if I hadn't used them the last two nights when she was up in the mortuary. I must have slept in my underclothes. Wonder why I hadn't worried so these last two nights?

Probably it was all from the strain of the funeral and the inquest.

I made up the bed before the fire.

And I was surprised the next morning that I had slept so well.

XXXI

It was the phone bell that awoke me.

Doreen, I remember saying, answer it will you? Then I fully awoke and realised that it was not the extension by the bed which was ringing. Which Doreen had always answered, for the phone was on her side.

This was the bell from the hall.

It was morning, daylight. The phone bell ringing shrill from the hall.

And no Doreen to answer it.

A patient cancelling her appointment for that morning.

Shall I fix up another date I asked?

She made an excuse and then rang off.

My three appointments for that morning cancelled. Neither did they make another appointment.

This was something I had not foreseen.

My patients going away with the leg.

That day I passed in going through my accounts and preparing some of my bills ready to be sent out.

And during that day messages came in to cancel practically all my engagements for that week and the weeks following. People of the town phoned up and spoke quietly but curtly. From the country came little notes handed in at the front door. I could see the boy or girl who brought the note trying to peer past me down into the hallway.

The evening mail brought several more cancellations. Quite calmly I took it all. The disappearance of my living.

Not that I minded overmuch. For I had never loved dentistry. Always it had been to me something forced on a son by a father. By a father who was determined to be elevated himself by seeing his son in a chosen profession.

I could live without the money which my work brought in. For I had sufficient invested to keep me in comparative comfort for the rest of my life.

The next few days were the most peaceful I have spent in the whole of my life. The nights I slept by the fire in the kitchen, snug and warm.

The daytime I only went out to buy groceries, such few as I needed. The rest of the time I spent in the house. And now, looking back and remembering, I try to recall what I did in those days. But I can remember little.

In the mornings I stayed in bed late. In the evenings I went to bed very early.

The house was quiet, very quiet. Seldom even did I hear the singing of the boy next door now.

And with the quiet came the dust. So much of it that at first I felt frightened. For I had never seen so much before. Then I realised that I was living in a house that was never dusted. I remembered how each morning, while I was working in the surgery at the front of the house, she would be hobbling around the rest of the house, a yellow duster in her hand. And with it she would be mopping up the dust from the shelves and the furniture, carrying it outside and shaking it out there to the wind.

Dust, the dirty dishes and the growing pile of embers in the grate; those my memories of those days.

And after a time difficulties began to arise.

Shillings for the gas. Money to pay the milkman at the end of the week. The coal too was getting low.

I never knew quite for how long I lived like this. But it could have been for a few days only.

I was very happy.

Until the day came that there was the very heavy knock on the front door.

XXXII

It frightened me that knock. It was different.

The first thought that came to me was that perhaps they had found out. That knock seemed so official, severe. Different from the other knocks that had come during the past few days from the callers cancelling the appointments. This knock was heavy and certain. As if it was essential that I should answer it.

I moved into the hall from the kitchen and paused a moment there, one hand on the hallstand.

Let them knock again.

The second time it was heavier. And with the knock came a ring of the day bell also. And with it I could hear too the fainter ring from upstairs as the night bell was also rung.

Impatient this caller.

I slowly opened the door, holding the edge carefully in both my hands.

Even as I opened it the voice called out that it was the railways parcels van, parcel for Mr Sterrill.

Goods? I hadn't ordered anything.

Then I remembered.

The leg. Something had gone wrong.

The uniformed carter was lifting the box down from the back of the square van.

Yes, it was the leg all right. I knew the shape. But not my box.

Hope came that perhaps it was the duplicate that we had ordered long ago. But that hope went as I remembered that Doreen had cancelled the order. Cancelled it because she had grown so used to *that* leg that she could not bear the thought of using another.

The man was carrying the box towards me.

'In the hall, sir?' he asked, and I just nodded. He carried it in and set it against the wall.

I signed the form as he asked and shut the door after him. Listened to the purr of his motor as he moved his van on down the street. Moved on and away, leaving me with the new wooden box which contained . . .

I read the label to make sure.

It was from them all right.

But I must make sure. A sudden panic, a fever to know came to me and I remember that I ran with the box into the surgery.

Once in there I laid it across the dusty arms of the dental chair. I clawed and scratched at the lid with my bare hands to open the nailed-on top. My one finger was bleeding and it was the drop of red blood falling on to the white wood of the case which slowed me up.

But I must see, I must open the box. Open it to find out what was inside it.

I prised up the lid with a pair of dental forceps. Half the nickel-plated handle broke. I threw it away and carried on with another. I would never need them again. For never again would I extract teeth.

With the loud squeak of the nails coming out of the tight wood, I pulled off the lid.

Inside a level lawn of sawdust. Another drop of blood fell from my hand and was lost in the soggy sawdust.

A small letter there, an envelope lying on top. A type-written address, for me.

I took up the envelope, and opened it.

Inside a letter. Quite a short one. Just to say that the firm had no use for second-hand legs. That all such aids were made to measure and fitted to the individual. Hence I would appreciate that the leg would fit one person only. With regret they returned the leg.

So it had come back.

The battle was on again.

XXXIII

The next week I moved from Welton. I placed all my furniture on sale at the local auction rooms, holding back only a few personal things.

I let my house.

Then I made arrangements with an inn about thirty miles away up in the hills. A quiet place where I had once stayed in my student days. I took the sole use of a small room there with all my meals and attendance for an all-in fee.

There I would find perhaps some small peace and relaxation.

For I had left the leg behind in Welton. In the small cupboard under the stairs, the entrance to which I had carefully covered over with wallpaper.

I felt almost free that day as I left Welton to take up my abode at the inn in the hills. The inn which has been my home since then and from which I write this, the story of my life.

XXXIV

I told them at the inn that I had had a nervous break-down. They understood in a vague sort of way and were kind enough to me, leaving me strictly alone as I had asked.

The days I would spend walking over the sheep tracks, thinking always of what had been.

The only time I really forgot her – and it – was in the evenings. Then I would go down to the public bar and join in with the locals who came in at night from the surrounding farms. Darts was our chief game. And in the excitement of a darts match I often forgot for quite a long time what I had known in the past. Forgot too the dread of what I knew was waiting for me someday.

Little to say about those first days at the inn. Except that I was always quite sure that the leg would catch up with me. My sleep was always deep and happy. But before I went to bed each night, I prayed that the good Lord would watch over me and keep the thing away from me for the night and one day longer.

Just for one night and one day, Lord, I prayed.

Little mail came to me at the inn. Except that which

was sent on from Welton. Bills and the necessary information about my house and practice.

Then came the letter. From my tenants.

Quite briefly to say that the fourth step on the stairs had collapsed one evening as the husband was going up to bed. His foot had gone right through and landed on something metallic. With the aid of a torch he had investigated. He had found the leg. He was sending it on to me.

His P.S. said that he was arranging to have the stairway repaired. He would send on the bill.

XXXV

The leg arrived on the bus.

The driver carried it off the top of the old square motor-coach, with its little edge of railing around the roof to hold the country parcels.

I was waiting for it. There were only two buses per day passing the inn. And I knew that it would be with the evening bus that it must come.

And wrapped in brown paper this time.

The man carried it into the front door of the pub. I gave him sixpence. With a slight touch of his greasy peaked cap he left me to go back to his bus, the country people inside staring at me as I stood there at the door of the inn with the thing in my arms.

At the toe the paper had torn a little and the metal rounded end of the toe showed through. They had wrapped it very roughly in lengths of old newspaper and oddments of brown paper covering the whole. It was criss-crossed and bound tight with hairy twine sinking deep into the paper layers.

The landlord offered to carry it up for me. But I said no, I would carry it myself.

Up in my little room I unpacked it.

It looked just the same as ever. But dusty now and with one of the buckles of the harness beginning to rust a little. Otherwise – just the same.

What now?

I must think. I could not do with it here in my room.

The landlord, his cellar.

I went down to see him in his kitchen. He was there with a pipe to wait the opening time at the bar. I told him that I had had an artificial leg sent to me by a friend as a joke. There was hardly room up there in my room for it. Could I store it down in the cellar among his barrels?

He said yes, certainly. But he looked at me queerly.

We carried it down there, the two of us. Down the rough worn stone steps to the cellar. The landlord going first, carrying the foot.

He knew his way in the darkness of the top steps. Then he dropped his end of the leg and he switched on the light.

I was surprised at the size of the cellar. It ran under the whole of the house. The barrels neatly stacked around the walls, the ones in use standing on trestles in the centre, the pipes leading from them up to the bar above.

Quite a few bottles too in the cellar, showing dark on racks against the white-washed walls.

The electric bulb was on the end of a long cable and hanging from a hook.

The landlord took it down and turned it from side to side, arcing long shadows around as he moved the lamp, looking for a clear spot to leave the leg.

At last we found an empty cask in the one corner, its top staved in. We stood the leg in this and the landlord told me that the barrel wouldn't be going back for some time so the leg would be all right in there, sir. Best to put it out of sight the man said. It would startle the women if they should happen to come down here at night-time and see the thing.

It would indeed, good landlord. It would indeed.

XXXVI

My dreams came back.

Starting as they had done long ago.

For it was under the same roof as me . . .

It was not yet destroyed.

But I had a plan. Better than any I had had before to lose the leg. As clever a plan to get rid of *it* as my plan had been to get rid of *her*.

XXXVII

The second night after the arrival of the leg at the inn I started to put my plan into action.

At twelve thirty that night I arose. I say arose, but I had not really been to bed. I had just sat there reading in the quiet of my bedroom. Downstairs the last customers had gone with turning-out time. And after that I could hear the clink of glasses from the bar as the maid collected in the glasses and the mugs. The noise of the cash till being emptied out on the counter and the money being counted. And the other sounds as of any other house being put to bed. The slamming of the doors and the fastening of the bolts. Then the faint rattle as the landlord then tried them to see if they held firm. The winding of the clocks, the one in the hall and the one in the bar. The goodnights to the maid. The soft thud in the yard below my window as the cat was put out for the night, its squawk of anger giving way to silence as it prowled off into the night.

All this as I sat there reading.

Luck had it that the lavatory of the house was on the ground floor. Luck for me so that if anyone caught me prowling downstairs, I was safe. Safe to be on the ground floor. But after that . . .?

Downstairs?

For I was going to the cellar . . .

The cellar door opened just by the side of the kitchen door. The latter was a fancy affair with a brass shiny knob and a coloured door-plate. At the top a small square of cathedral glass to colour the upper panel.

But the cellar door was as old as the house itself. Old dark oak with a lift-up latch to open.

I prayed before the cellar door.

Prayed as if I was entering some sacred place. For it seems to me that it is more necessary to pray to God when on the way to meet the devil than it is when going to face God himself.

And so I prayed . . .

Then I lifted the latch and swung open the door.

The faint smell of wood and of old stale beer came up from the blackness.

Two steps down to reach the light switch.

Two steps only . . . one step . . . two steps.

The switch. Where?

To the right . . . or the left?

I felt to the right, smoothing my shaking fingers over the rough whitewash of the cellar wall. A little of the lime-wash came away as I rubbed it and I could hear the noise as the light flakes fell in the quiet, onto the floor of the cellar, many feet below. I reached out further to my left. To feel that switch, that raised knob, to press it down. I passed my fingers, then my hand, and lastly my whole arm in an arc over the wall seeking for the switch. At the very length of the arc, my fingers touched a soft clinging mass of cobwebs.

I drew in my arm. Stood there breathing heavy on the quiet steps. The switch was not on my left. And yet I could have sworn that I had seen it there when we had gone down before.

The right then? Try there.

Rough beams of wood here along the plaster.

The switch fastened on to one of the wooden beams.

The strong yellow light on and I felt better. On down the rest of the steps and shutting the door behind me. Stepping over the mallets and wedges used to tap the barrels.

Across the cellar floor and to the hanging bulb. Reach it down, hold it in my hand. Then I felt afraid again. For although in front of me all was bright light. Behind was . . . darkness.

I kept turning around, swinging the bright bulb behind me. But that was worse. All the moving shadows.

But at last I got up to the tub. Which one? A row of six barrels there?

Panic again? Which one?

The one without a top, you idiot. Of course. I flashed the light inside. The leg was still there. Lengths of grey cobwebs inside the cask, with the sides too covered with yellow fungus and green mould.

I must work quickly.

Looking back now I think that those moments in the cellar were among the worst that I spent after the night I watched Doreen die.

Hooking the lamp to a nail I started to work. To get the cask to look like the other empty ones . . . To fix on the lid, the displaced boards.

It was easier than I had expected. The timber was not broken at all, only just pushed in.

I straightened them. A quick look at my work in the light of the lamp. And then my nerves completely and utterly gave way again.

I ran with the lamp to the centre of the cellar. Hung up the bulb on to its hook and then ran for the cellar steps, up and snapped off the light switch.

Darkness.

The latch of the door. Where was it?

I had to switch on the light again to find the latch.

Then out with the light again, open the cellar door, out into the hallway.

Safe again.

The house all quiet. Only the tick from the big clock in the hallway. And the quiet creak as its long brass pendulum slowly swung.

All quiet. But to make sure, to make sure just in case someone had heard my going . . . I must use the lavatory . . .

Then up the stairs. To my bedroom.

I feared to sleep that night. For I had attacked the leg and I was afraid that it might now attack me. Attack me in the only way possible, in my sleep, in my dreams.

But that night I slept well. Very well.

And I was almost gay the next morning when the landlord told me that the brewers were coming that very day to collect their empties.

'Your leg, sir? Shall I get it for you?'

'No, no,' I said. 'I'll get it, I know the way, you're a busy man.'

He said it was all right by him and so I went down to the cellar, looked again at my cask to see that all was well. Then I waited until I heard the landlord walking heavy about in the bar overhead. And then I quietly slipped up from the cellar and through the hall. And walked heavy up the stairs to my room.

XXXVIII

The brewers' lorry came about midday. It was a long, heavy lorry towing a large trailer. Around the edges of the lorry and the trailer were guarding lengths of chain fastened to large upright iron stanchions.

I went down to the doorway of the inn as the lorry braked to a standstill on the quiet yard by the side of the country road.

Barrels there on the lorry and on the trailer. I asked the man how they knew which barrels were full, which were empty? He told me that they placed the empties on the trailer and the full ones were unloaded from the lorry itself. We have a system, sir, he said.

The landlord had gone down to the cellar to open up the big wooden doors, usually flush with the surface of the yard. One of the men with the lorry had taken off a long ladder-like appliance which they kept tucked away under the oily back axle. Shaped like a ladder, but that the rungs were curved.

The landlord called up through the doors, 'Send the full ones down and I'll send up the empties afterwards. I've only got a few today.'

The man on the lorry rolled a barrel to the edge of the lorry. Then placed the cask edgeways on the ladder and let it slide gently to the floor. Then they rolled it to the cellar entrance. There they placed the ladder from the yard down into the cellar. To the edges of the barrel they fixed a Y-shaped rope, the arms of the Y fastened to the rims of the barrel. Then they quietly slid the barrels down into the cellar. The man in there with the landlord taking the weight off the man holding the rope above. Then I could hear the two of them rolling the barrel across the cellar floor and putting it into position.

The same with all the other full barrels which they were going to leave at the inn that day.

'The empties next,' called out the driver.

The empties . . .

Now for it.

In the cellar the landlord and the driver's mate were rolling up the empties to the cellar opening.

So far all was well. Nothing had gone wrong. They would have heard if the leg had rattled or anything . . . a weakness that. I should have packed it around . . . but they would have heard if it had rattled.

Now they were hauling the barrels up. One by one. Fixing the two arms of the rope to the edges of the barrel. Then the man up above hauling the empties up with a rush up the skids of the ladder.

Two, three. Four barrels. A dozen.

'Only one more,' called out the landlord.

Only one more.

'Baker's dozen,' called out the driver.

Just one more.

And was the one with the thing in it up here among the twelve? Or was it that one down there? That one still to come?

But only the one. It would soon be over for there was only that one to come up.

But the man pulling up the barrel, he slipped on a loose coil of rope. The barrel was up halfway. He let the rope go and it slid through his hands and although he quickly recovered himself and the rope, it was too late. One of the arms of the rope had come off the barrel and it swung round to the one side and rolled back to the cellar floor.

'Look out,' shouted the driver. The men in the cellar jumped aside to let the barrel roll on past them and rebound against the far wall.

I waited.

For I knew, knew even as it fell, I knew that it was the one containing the leg.

I knew too that it had opened and that my secret had been discovered. For there was a little chatter from the cellar and the landlord's rather red face appeared at the bottom of the ladder.

'Mr Sterrill,' he called. 'You've left your leg in the barrel by mistake.'

I made some mad excuse and then ran from the three and into the house.

As I left them I could hear the landlord saying something about nervous breakdown . . . memory . . .

And I felt the pitying stare of the driver of the brewers' lorry at my back as I left. The little clatter too, I heard as the driver's mate climbed the ladder, doubtless to have a last look at me.

The landlord carried the thing back up to my room when the lorry had gone. He said that he was sorry about my absent-mindedness which had caused me to leave the leg in the barrel. 'You take things easier, sir,' the man said. 'Let the missus and me do the worrying for you. It's a good thing too, sir, that you didn't leave that leg of yours in the barrel. They would sure have discovered it inside when they went to scald out the inside at the brewery, and it would have been very awkward to explain.'

I thanked the man. He asked me should he store the leg again in the cellar?

I said no, don't bother. Leave it with me . . .

XXXIX

That afternoon I took the bus into the small market town two miles away. A quiet unmoving place, lying in a sort of bowl among the hills.

It was fair day. The farmers and the dealers standing in little clumps around the streets, talking business.

With me I had the leg.

In the bus I had laid it along the length of the luggage rack. But the conductor had called out. Very loudly, so that all in the single-decker bus could plainly hear.

'Whose is that parcel? This parcel, who does it belong to?'

I was startled. So sudden a question to ask. A parcel, why surely this man must see hundreds of parcels in a week? Why must he ask so loudly?

Perhaps it was the shape?

I called out to him: 'Mine and why do you ask?'

He said back: 'Acid spilt there from a wireless battery. You'll have to move your parcel, sir.'

I moved it and stuck it between my knees.

Alighting in the market town I walked down the High

Street carrying the leg under my arm, the point jutting forward.

I knew my way well around this little place. For I had visited it quite often from my home on bicycle rides, when I was a boy.

Sharp left by the school and down the lane to the gasworks.

The gasworks?

I, a dentist, heading for the gasworks in a small Welsh market town?

It was the furnace I wanted.

For I had heard that in gasworks the furnaces are very, very hot and that they would shrivel tins and metal to smoke in a few seconds.

And my leg was metal.

But there they would have none of it.

The furnace man referred me to the manager. He asked lots of questions. A bald man he was, with a little grey fringe of hair over his ears. And all the time while I spoke to him he was smoking a large pipe which he relit constantly from a pile of Swan matches lying on his desk. He wanted to know all about the leg. But I told him little. He was not the kind of man I could confide in. He talked in rather a high-pitched voice and he was quite certain in all he said. The only people who were allowed to destroy anything in the furnaces were the police. Those were his instructions he said. Perhaps I would care to see the police?

My God, the police!

I believe he thought that I was quite mad for he kept watching the leg which I held all the time, under my arm. His one hand too, rested on the phone as if he were about at any second to make a call. Several times too he asked me was the leg really artificial. I kept telling him all the time that it was but he seemed to doubt my word. He looked at my brown-paper parcel and sniffed the air a little at times. In the end I told him to tap the leg for himself to see that it was made of metal. But I added, for I knew well what a soul the thing had, the inside is real. That seemed to frighten the gasworks manager but I eventually persuaded him to tap the shaft of the leg with a heavy ruler. He seemed quite surprised at the hollow sound which came from the wrappings. And then he made me undo the wrappings to show the thing to him.

He laughed quite a lot when he saw that the leg was made of metal. 'Why, old man,' he said, 'I thought that you wanted to turn our place into a crematorium or something. You take that thing to the police and tell 'em about it.'

His hand was off the phone now.

'But,' he added, 'perhaps you'd better see a doctor first.'

I knew then that it was useless. That he would never let me have the use of his furnace.

And so I took the leg back to the inn . . .

XL

Back in my room I cried. In the bedroom I sobbed a long time, my face pushed into the soft comfortable pillows.

And that night I did not sleep. I waited for the dawn. Up there in that quiet bedroom. Alone in that house.

That night more than ever, the deep pity of my position came upon me. With all my heart I envied those to whom the night was nothing. A fleeting mind full of dreams and nothing, nothing more. Rest and refreshment. The quiet lost hours of the night.

But for me it was not so.

Sitting up there by my window looking out at the cold blue December night. Sometimes the light of a late car sweeping the hills on a distant hill road. Or the barking of some dog straining at its chain to get away into the night and to its mate.

The leg lying across the bottom of my bed, showing faintly pink in the glow from my bedside lamp. Up to now hatred had carried me on. But somehow, that night the whole terrible tragedy of my position came upon me. No one to love me. No one to care for me. No one to love and to care for.

She was gone. For Doreen had loved me, done those little things for me. But I had destroyed her to have my peace. It was too late now.

She was gone.

XLI

With the dawn I went out, out through the front door of the pub.

A misty cold morning it was, with faint yellow lights moving on the hillsides as the farmers went about the morning milk.

The leg I took with me, tucking it once again under my arm.

And then I started to walk the road, wet with dew. On into the hills.

As I walked the light grew stronger and I met a bicycle or two, labourers on their way to work. The postman and the milk lorries out to collect the milk.

I just walked on, along in the gravel at the side of the road, the thing held firmly under my right arm.

I do not know for how long I walked. It must have been for some hours. I remember little of the walk now, and the whole is a misty hazy memory in my mind. I know I walked through some small village.

It was as I was leaving the village, heading for the open country again . . .

For that last street was the street of my dreams . . .

The same quiet street which I knew so well, remembered so very clearly from those visions of the night.

The same houses with the steps up to them. The same lamp posts. The same road leading out into the distant country, the little brook and the little bridge. All there.

And it was the daytime that I walked this road.

All as the dream had told me.

I knew well what to do now.

I walked on past the last house, and into the open country. On until I reached the little bridge.

And there I undid the parcellings of the leg. Cold and grey it looked in the light of the winter afternoon.

I caught hold of it by the pointed toe and raised it high above my head like an axe. Then brought it crashing down on the hard road.

It broke at the knee. The thigh I took and held by the straps, banging it down on the brick parapet of the culvert. The metal slowly dented and flattened. Then I threw it far up into the muddy water of the flooded brook. It fell with a splash and the water spurted out over the green grass of the meadow.

The lower portion I broke by hitting it again and again on the road. Then I flattened it by stamping on it. After that I threw it away up the stream, away and opposite to the thigh portion.

The foot I heaved into a small clump of rushes at the bottom of the little bridge.

I looked around me. There was nothing left, nothing. It was totally destroyed.

But . . . it was not as it should be. I was not at ease. I remembered the dream. As I walked back up the road I knew something was missing. The old man, that was it, the old man who had pointed. Where was he?

Halfway up that gentle slope I stopped. I needed no old man to tell me, to point. I looked round, turning my head very quickly. The one look was enough. It was following me as I knew it would. Hopping gently along on its toe and swaying just a little from side to side.

XLII

Halfway back to the inn it caught up with me.

Every so often I had looked round, all the while it was gradually becoming nearer to me. By the late afternoon it was walking beside me, keeping in step with me as I walked along.

It was on my left side and I could hear its faint gentle tapping on the hard road surface.

Few cars came to pass me. But as they came towards me I lowered my head so as not to face those who may be looking. For what could I say to explain? And at every passing bicycle I stooped to fasten my shoelace.

But it stooped too.

Some of the men passing said good evening to me as I bent down. But I kept silent and as soon as they had passed me I carried on walking quickly for the inn.

It was evening when I got back there.

The landlord was just opening the bar when I got in.

'We've missed you, Mr Sterrill,' he said to me. I told him that I had been away to take the leg back to the man who had played the joke on me.

The landlord said that he was sure that he was glad that

the thing had gone back. 'Kind of grows on a man, sir,' he said. 'Anyway, it's with its rightful owner now, sir.'

I said yes and looked down at my side.

The thing was standing there, perched on its toe, and still swaying from side to side, very gently.

With its rightful owner at last?

XLIII

The words of an old curse, Irish I believe, have been in my mind of late:

> *May your body be a boat and your ribs*
> *oars to ferry you to hell . . .*

I was on the way all right.
Every day I was getting nearer.
And all the time it was with me.

As I ate my meal that night on returning from the country it watched from an easy chair.

The maid who brought in the food laid it as she had always done. Nothing unusual. Nothing wrong.

I spoke to her. 'Lucy,' I said. 'Do you notice anything different in this room?'

She looked around. At the pictures on the wall, the table, the floor.

At the easy chair.

'Nothing, sir,' the girl said. 'Except that the salt is half empty, sir. Shall I fill it?'

'No, don't bother now, Lucy,' and with that I sent her away.

It's for you alone, you fool. You alone it's waiting. It's not interested in anybody else, except you, you who murdered its mistress.

As I ate my meal I watched the chair.

It had taken up the position as any leg attached to a human frame would have done. The thigh part resting on the seat of the chair. I could even see where the soft felt of the material sank a little. The knee crooked to a right angle and the calf parallel to the upright part of the chair.

And sometimes as I watched the toe would tap the floor a little, like an impatient woman, waiting.

I went down quickly after dinner, down to the bar room to have a game with whoever might be there.

I hoped that perhaps the leg would stay up in my room, although the thought of having to leave the gay lighted tap-room after the evening was over, to have to go up to that thing in my rooms, frightened me.

But it came with me to the bar, dodging in between the customers, and finally settling on the other side of the bar, on the small keg of spirit which was kept there.

I stayed in the bar until closing time and all the customers had gone.

The landlord looked at me as I sat there in the corner by the dying fire.

'Never seen you stay so late, Mr Sterrill,' he said.

I told him that I was feeling a little gloomy and he offered to bring me up some whisky. I said yes, for I was glad to have any company come up there to me.

Upstairs.

I knew it was following me. When I opened the bedroom door there was a ghastly second before I switched on the light. In that second I could feel it hopping past me. When I switched on the light it was already in the room sitting there on the easy chair.

And as I watched the toe reared itself up in the air. Out and across, as if that leg were crossing another unseen leg.

It was then that the landlord brought me my whisky.

The man put the mug down by my bedside. Carefully placing it so that none of the liquor spilled over onto the coloured linen covering the bedside table.

'Nothing else you require, sir?'

'Nothing,' I said. 'Nothing at all.'

'If you're feeling ill, Mr Sterrill, we can always get a doctor.'

'Do I look ill?' I asked him.

He just nodded. Then 'Well, sir, not ill, really it's kind of frightened you look. It worries me and the wife, sir. Only, mark you, it's none of our business.'

I sipped the hot whisky.

'Nothing you can see wrong then, in this room for example, landlord?'

He looked around the room with his quiet slow eyes. Looked at each wall in turn, then into the corners.

'Nothing, sir, just the same as usual, sir. Why, Mr Sterrill?'

'Well, I seem to be seeing things. I suppose it's my nerves, losing my wife you know. Only it's very frightening up here in this quiet room to feel that there is something with one.'

'No need to be afraid, sir. We all gets that feeling at different times in our life, sir. That there's something with us. But we just carries on with our work and forgets all about it. Forgets all about it in the business of making a living. Pity you couldn't get out of yourself more, Mr Sterrill. Forget yourself for a while.'

'That's what I've been trying to do, landlord.'

God knows that's what I've been trying to do . . .

'But don't be frightened, sir. You can always call and we'll hear you right away. The wife and I sleep just across the corridor as you know, sir. Just call out – but I'll tell you what, Mr Sterrill, I'll bring you a small handbell so that you can ring out in the night and be sure to wake us up if you want to.'

He went out.

It was still sitting there, its toe slightly off the ground.

The landlord came back with an old heavy large brass handbell.

'It's the one that the auctioneers use when they have the sales in the yard, sir. Why, with this, sir, you could wake the dead themselves.'

'God forbid, landlord.'

'Ay sir, God forbid. Well, I'll be off to bed, sir. If you like, sir, I'll leave the cat with you. He's real company is Fidio. He's an affectionate thing, Mr Sterrill, and purrs if you just look at him.'

The man went out again and brought in a large black cat in his arms. He dropped it on the floor and it came across towards me, arching its back and purring.

'Thanks, landlord. Fidio will be great company to me.'

At the door the landlord turned and looked around at me.

'Mr Sterrill, if I may say so, sir, religion is an excellent thing if you think that things are with you, sir. You take my advice and go to church on Sunday.'

With that he said goodnight and was gone.

My God, what a grand idea.

Church on Sunday!

XLIV

I have always believed that in cats there is something of the hidden subtle power of Satan. The way they walk so quietly but change when need arises. The affected purr for those whom it pays them to love and their cruel ways with those they have in their power.

So I rather doubted the black cat that the host gave me for company.

It was still rubbing itself against my pyjama leg and I noticed with distaste that some of its long black hairs were adhering to the silk of my pyjamas. I sent it away and it slunk off still purring. Slunk away to the chair.

What came next was interesting. As the cat drew near the leg swung back over itself as if it were a normal figure uncrossing its legs. Then as the cat came near to the chair the leg hopped up and away into a dark corner of the room where there was little glow from my bedside lamp.

But the leg was not lost to sight. For from the thing there came a faint glow. But not a rosy glow as of health. But a greenish-brown glow.

And I remembered so very well that colour. The colour of the body which a medical student had taken me to see in my Varsity days. The body which had been found in a little bed in a quiet room in a back street.

A body which should have been buried long ago.

But the thing feared that cat. And I remember all the tales which they told in the country district of why always the windows of the room in which lay a corpse, why always these windows were kept *closed*. The country folk said that the cats could smell a corpse from miles and would try to break into the house for the feast . . .

Yes, the thing feared the cat that night. I could see that. For as the cat went to sleep rolled up on that chair which was the favourite of the thing, well, it just stayed far away in the corner. With that faint glow coming from all over it, lest I should forget.

But the presence of Fidio gave me much comfort. Its soft breathing reassured me. The handbell too gave me confidence that I could wake the whole household with one movement of that heavy carved handle.

But the cat and the bell didn't do away with the fact that the leg was still in my vision. There with that glow of decay and putrefication coming from it.

Strange it was then that sleep came so soon. Perhaps it was the whisky and the confidence arising from the cat and the handbell. Or maybe it was just that I was very exhausted from my walk.

But that night I did sleep exceedingly well. No dreams in the hours of the night.

I awoke feeling much refreshed. And I do believe that that morning for the first few seconds I quite forgot the existence of the thing.

But for a few seconds only. I looked at the handle of the handbell and remembered why I had it. I looked then at the chair. The thing was seated there, twisting around on itself. For all the world as if a woman were sitting there with her one leg twisted under her. Sitting on her leg as many women do. Doreen had sat hours like that before she lost her leg.

My cat, Fidio? Where was he? If he were in the chair there would be no leg there.

But Fidio was sitting happy on the sun-blistered windowsill, pawing out at a big bluebottle buzzing there in the faint winter sunshine.

XLV

Sunday.

Day of Rest. Just that to most people. Simply a day of rest.

But that Sunday meant more to me than that, another Seventh Day.

For although I had been brought up very religiously, yet I, like most sons of religious parents, had turned my back on religion the moment I had my choice.

I don't think that I had been to church once since that summer day when Doreen and I were wed. Not once.

But it was to church that my thoughts turned that winter's morning. Christmas coming near and the farmers on the little hill farms were penning up the geese ready for the final fattening.

I decided to go to church that Sunday morning. It was my hope, my salvation perhaps, that the church could save me from the Thing which haunted and followed me. Which seemed a very part of my being.

Lying there that Sunday morning, the little sash windows opaque with frost, I watched the leg. And thought of the stories I had heard. How once, long ago it had been the duty of the church to 'lay ghosts'. And to keep away evil spirits by signs and the use of holy water. I thought how a little odd it was that those in love with Satan needed no evil water or signs of hell to keep away God. Satan looked after his own quite well I thought . . .

But perhaps the wonderful atmosphere of a parish church would protect me. The aroma there after all the centuries of worship, honest worship too, of these country folk. Perhaps, perhaps the thing would not come there? To stand before God's altar . . . For if it could come there . . . if she could come there, then the very mansions of heaven must be open to Satan, who was her master, even as she was master of this thing snug on the cloth felt of the easy chair.

Then I remembered a frightful story I had once read. Of a more godly man than I, a vicar, who had been haunted even as I was, by a something. And as this good man was celebrating the Holy Communion the thing appeared before the communion table and spilled the holy wine.

Would I then, sinner, be safe?

Try.

Matins it must be. The morning service. It must be that.

I quickly dressed and let the cat out of the room. The maid brought in my breakfast and as she left the room I told her that I would be rather late for lunch. I said I was going to church that morning. The girl seemed surprised at that. For the morning sun had gone and from the heavy clouds coming in from the west a few flakes of snow were already falling.

I set out to the village.

It was with me. On my left side. Just hopping quietly along.

By now it was snowing quite heavily. Dry powdery stuff that kicked up into fine spray as we walked along.

We?

I looked down at it.

It left no footprints in the snow . . .

Only it and me walking along. Oh, a white Christmas it would be. The children would be happy and in the towns the holly and the mistletoe would be selling fast. The GPO would be busy and everybody, even those lonely ones with no loved ones, even they would catch the spirit of Christmas and make this a special time, a different time, a happier time. And for me? No Christmas decorations. How Doreen had wobbled on the top of the steps but wouldn't let me pin up the streamers and the coloured paper. Always said that it was unlucky for a man to do it. And so I had just held the step ladder and waited like a partner in an acrobat act, in case she should come tumbling down, I to catch her. No Xmas cards for me either. Perhaps the tenants would send one?

Only it and me walking along, I kicking up the snow. Sometimes a car would pass, driving carefully. Then we would walk in the print of the tyres for it was easier to walk there. But soon the marks would be snowed over and it would be smooth, deepening snow all the time.

I was speaking.

'It won't last long. It's coming down too thick.'

God help me, I was talking to it.

Supposing, supposing that it, there in the quiet of the snows of that country road, supposing it should answer me . . . speak to me . . .

Please God, I'm going to your House. Don't let it talk to me. Just one chance, God, just one chance . . .

The church was on a small hill above the village.

An old tired-looking building, grey now against the snow. With the beeches and the old firs around the walls. By one side and screened from it by a row of tall poplars was the vicarage, a large square house, big and desolate, like the one I had been born in.

The snow was clearing a little and as we walked past the vicarage I could see the red glow of the fire, the small old-fashioned panes with their twisted glass giving a distorted view of the inside.

Happy man of the church. If only I had taken that road, as my mother had wished.

Leaning against the walls of the churchyard were one or two bicycles, their seats carefully covered with old sacks to keep off the snow.

I opened the iron wicket of the path leading up into the churchyard. The snow clogged the gate a little so that I had to push it hard to open. And as I opened it, it skidded a small pile of snow to the side with the bottom bar. Others had gone before. I could see their faint imprints in the snow.

I held the gate open as for a dog to come through.

The leg hopped into the churchyard.

I closed the gate again.

Up we walked through the graves, the snow in white layers on top of the grey stones. Giving a white cap to the glass tops of the everlasting wreaths.

Up to the porch of the old church.

I was watching it very carefully now, my companion.

It was as I stepped over the slate slab at the porch entrance that it left me.

The joy of that moment. The sheer joy to look around inside the porch, look at the dark oak walls and to see that it was gone. To see the lists of sidesmen pinned to the green baize of the noticeboard and the lists of the voters. The results of the collections and the notices of the church socials. I lingered by that green noticeboard and fingered the brass drawing pins. Such ordinary little things, bought in Woolworths probably. Wonder had they been consecrated?

But I must experiment.

I stepped to the edge of the porch again.

The snow was falling heavy again and the village below was hidden.

By the step of the porch I paused.

Would it come back to me?

I stepped out onto the white pathway, up to my ankles in the snow.

I looked to my left side.

It was there.

I stepped back into the porch.

I was alone again.

So I had at last found a place where it could not reach me.

From the tower above a bell began to peal. So I had a few minutes before the service began. One or two people passed me. Looked curiously at me as I lingered there in the porch.

At last I went right in, pushing aside the small inner door.

Once inside I looked to my side again. I half expected to see it there once again. But I was still free.

I sat in a pew halfway down the church. Sat there utterly happy through the service, wishing that it was longer, far longer.

It was only a short sermon. And the old white-haired clergyman mumbled a lot to himself. But one phrase remained with me. It was a quotation which he said was from Schiller: *Abide not alone, for it was in the desert that Satan came to the Lord of Heaven himself.*

Outside the leg was waiting for me and we walked back together to the inn.

XLVI

The next day I went into the village again. By now the snow was covering the countryside evenly and deeply. So that the fields were shown only by the black tops of their hedges and it was impossible to tell which was ploughed land, which was pasture. The buses had stopped running and so I had to walk all the way.

The upper part of the snow had frozen into a hard crust. Quite firm but not strong enough to support me. I sank in with every step. But the leg, I noticed, seemed to skim over the top of the snow.

I went to the church again. Into the porch.

An old man was there sweeping away the snow. He said he was the verger and he was very anxious to show me a skeleton which he had down in the vaults.

But I said that I was a doctor and that skeletons meant nothing to me, they were my living I told him. He seemed pleased at that and seemed to regard me as having something in common with him. Kept rubbing his hands and saying, beautiful things, beautiful things.

Then he offered to take me around the outside and

point out the blocked-up Norman arch. But I said no, it was the *inside* of the church that I wanted to see.

At that he propped up his broom against the oak panels of the porch and took me around the inside of the church.

He showed me the font which he said was fashioned from the base of a pillar said to be taken from the old Cistercian abbey which had stood in a fold of the hills, by the river. He showed me too the pulpit which, with the communion table, dated from the time of Queen Elizabeth.

A wonderful old man this. When he forgot about his skulls and his skeletons his love of that old church was wonderful to see. My church he kept on saying, my church.

We talked on and on in quiet voices in that lovely old building.

'Tell me, friend,' I said to the sexton, 'tell me, where in the village can I buy a Bible. Just a small plain Bible. I have come from town rather in a hurry and now I'm without one.'

'Forgot your Bible, *sir*.'

He then told me of a small shop in the village, a kind of universal stores where they sold Bibles.

I went out sadly from the church, saying goodbye to my friend the verger, for it was getting late and I did not fancy the walk home along the roads, in the snow, with only the leg for company.

So we went down to the shop in the village.

It was a new Bible which I bought. With a shining, slightly sticky binding to it. The edges of the pages were coloured a bright red and as I opened to see the print the back gave a creak as it bent.

But I was glad of it.

I took it with me to the inn.

But it was of no use. The presence of Satan himself was stronger than the written word of God . . .

XLVII

The end is near.

It is Christmas Eve and the end is near.

That I know as I watch the thing this evening.

All the countryside is frost-bound hard and the snow is frozen deep. On the fields they have today been feeding the cattle, spreading out the hay on the top of the white snow. And here at the inn they have been wrapping pipes around with straw and sacking. And the landlord has lit a small fire by the outside pump to keep it from freezing.

If I go to the curtains and pull them aside with a whirr as they run the wire, I can see the still-glowing sticks of the fire. And even through the closed window comes the bitter smell of the burning straw.

Down in the taproom they have hung up the holly and there is mistletoe over the chimney. And I daresay that the barmaid is standing at the fire end of the counter, spreading out her red hands to the blaze, in between the serving.

Christmas Eve and the bustle and the starting of the cooking. The very smell of Christmas.

But I alone up here. My fire burns bright. My curtains are gay with their floral pattern. By turning the switch by my door I can make the room soft or strong with light.

It has been very restless tonight. Not sitting quiet but moving, all the time.

Moving about the room.

I have been writing much of this confession tonight. And all the time as I write it has been moving around me, taking tonight an *active* interest in me. Not just with me, but near and close to me all the time.

I stop writing. I will read the Bible. Try once again.

Always before it has failed. But maybe tonight? For it is Christmas . . .

With the Bible open on my knees I turn the pages. The Psalms. The twenty-third.

It was at the first words – *The Lord is My Shepherd* – that it happened.

I knew that the thing was moving up and down the length of the hearthrug. As I looked up the toe was in the air. And ever rising. Arising quietly but very straightly for the back of the Bible. A few seconds more and it would hit it . . .

I closed the Book. The leg descended once more.

Pity. The Psalm had been comforting too . . .

XLVIII

Later in the evening carol singers came. An organised party with a piano accordion, singing lustily at the main door below my bedroom. Men's voices mostly and well trained.

Pulling aside a corner of the curtain I watched them down there in the courtyard. They had cycle lamps fastened to their belts and they stood in a half-circle facing the door.

> *O come all Ye Faithful,*
> *Joyful and Triumphant,*
> *Come ye, O Come ye to Bethlehem . . .*

Sacred music this. Wonder how the leg was taking it.

It was doing a kind of polka to the music using the hearthrug as a floor. Keeping time to the music too. With the last verse it stopped and bent at the knee as if doing a little curtsey . . .

From the door came a little bustle as the landlord opened up to the singers. The clink of glass to glass as the men gave a toast to Xmas. Then they were gone, their cries of Merry Christmas, landlord, growing fainter. Only that to show they were going, for their footsteps were falling quiet in the snow.

Then It started to walk around in circles. Hopping around. Sometimes clockwise and sometimes anti-clockwise. When I sat in a chair it would move around and around me. Even when I moved across the room it would still move around me in circles.

There was not a moment that evening when it was quiet.

About midnight I started to sing. A hymn. One of the old, old hymns learnt at home, long ago.

There is a green hill far away . . .

It was then that the leg first started to hop to the door.
To the door and back again.
Quite suddenly I knew what it wanted me to do.
And try as I could I dare not resist it.
For the leg wanted me to follow. It was leading me.
Be brave, be strong, man and stay.
But I could not.
And so I followed it out and onto the landing.

XLIX

There in the soft glow from the low-wattage lamp I watched the leg.

It went along the landing and then hopped out between two of the banister rails.

Several times it did that. And then came back to me again, standing there in the doorway of my bedroom.

The last time it did this leap through the rails of the landing I went up to it, right to the edge. To see closer I switched on the normal lighting.

In the full light I saw that the leg was swinging by one of the harness straps. Swinging out there over the well of the stairs. Swinging gently to and fro.

I went back into the bedroom.

L

This will be the last chapter that I shall be allowed to write. My hours on this earth are coming to an end.

For it has told me what to do. The command has been given at last. Now all remains for me to do is but to obey.

These written words have given me some small comfort. They say confession is good for the soul. And at least that good kind man at the bank will remember me and feel perhaps a little pity for me. And it is good that that one man at least know how Doreen really died; and my story too.

The door onto the landing is ajar. The leg still swings there from the banisters.

The end is here.

My life may have been happy. But for the wet leaves on the road that night. *God works in a wondrous way his wonders to perform.* Ha, ha! Poor old God.

Old Satan doesn't do so badly either.

Ah well, I must go.

What the Bank Manager Thought

And as the bank manager closed the file he wondered why it had all been. Why all this had ever happened. Happened to that unassuming little dentist who had always been so quiet, steady, hard-working.

He wondered too, why the little man should have written all this out so carefully, so fully, and should have sent it to him, of all people, to read. Read it as near to Xmas as possible the pencilled note had said.

So he'd done it again this year. Strange how it all read so new each time.

And as he tied a length of tape around the file he wondered did they still close the inn over Christmas?

Still, it must have spoiled their fun to find him hanging from the banisters that Christmas morning.

Other Dark Tales

The Reflection

Jacques had always had the habit of looking at himself in a mirror. For quite a long time he would stare at the reflection of his thin face, tanned it was with the dark eyebrows and the long hooked nose.

He would stare unblinking his eyes at the eyes which looked back at him. Stare so long that the blue would become one long canal in which the bridge of his nose was lost.

Even while shaving Jacques would pause, the lather dripping off the end of his brush onto the cork floor of the bathroom. Little splashes of white on the blue design with its silver fishes. He would stare at himself and then would come the scream of his wife from the kitchen below. Telling him to hurry.

She always screamed in the morning. Then he would rub out the dropped lather off the floor with the leather sole of his slipper. For the marks would only make her the more difficult.

It was one morning while shaving that he first noticed it. The lather on the end of the shaving brush had been tinged with red. He had cut himself once again.

But looking at himself in the mirror there was no red blood on the whiteness of his shaved chin. Odd. He smoothed his hand over his chin. There it was, the long smear of blood on the inside of his palm.

Jacques did many odd little things like that in the week that followed. And it was always the mirrors.

He would spend the journey up to town in the morning staring at himself in the mirror in the first-class carriage. And in the lunch hour while out in the streets he would pause and stare at his reflection in the plate glass of the shop windows.

And at home in his own house Lucy said that he was quite, quite mad. For every evening he would take the big oval mirror from off the wall over the lounge fireplace. Take it off and prop it up on the polished tabletop. Then he would sit in a chair, chin on hands and watch himself reflected in the mirror.

Every night it was like that. Until the evening that Lucy said she was going out to fetch someone . . .

Tonight he had the idea. The wonderful idea. The wink, that proved it.

Jacques winked at himself. A long slow wink. Sometimes with his right eye. Sometimes with his left. But it was always the *other* which winked back. Ah well, she was out now. So now it must be.

The razor in his right hand. The steel glinted beautifully in the mirror. Pity he couldn't see it all as it really was.

Ah, Lucy was back. Good to see how the blood shocked her. And that doctor fellow from the end of the road. He was used to it alright. See how he lifted my chin right up to make quite sure?

The Man Who Walked On

He had built his house by the sea. A long, low house made from the grey stone of the only quarry on the island. And now, the rows of firs and pine which he had planted at that time, had grown high and tall at the back of the house. So that the front of his house opened right on to the shingle of the beach, and the back was hidden from the rest of the island by the trees.

He had lived here many years, coming the winter after she had been drowned.

Every night James walked from the door on the leeward side of his house, down through the wiry marram grass and on to the big stones at the high-water line. Summer and winter, just at the time of sunset, he would walk out and always down to the very waves of the sea. Sometimes a long walk, when the tide was low, and his feet leaving the imprints in the hard wet sand. Sometimes too, when the tide was high, especially in January, the sea almost reached his garden, and the walk would then be short.

But always he let the water touch the leather of his boots.

It was one October evening he noticed it. The tide had been low at sunset and James had had to walk far to reach the last waves of the sea. So far out that looking back he could see around the island. And to the darkening mountains of the mainland.

It was night when he turned to walk back. And there was only the moan of the sea as it sucked back through the straits, and the call of the wild duck on the marshlands on the west side of the island. The only noise that, and the thump of his boots on the wet sand. The wet sand left in little ripples by the ebbing waves.

The harvest moon was rising. Out of the sea at the back of him, lighting up the island and showing the dark trees at the back of his house, and the gleam of its slates, wet in the evening dew.

James walked home towards his house, dodging the pools of water and the white patches of shell, for he hated the crunching so. On his way home he walked, back from the edge of the sea.

Then he noticed it. It should have been in front of him. Blacker even than the darkness of the sand.

God in Heaven, it should be there, clear in all this moonshine, there in front of him, his shadow?

They took him away from his stone house by the seashore. Took him away, the two men on either side of him, away, and in a boat to the mainland. And there they took him to the big house with the barred gate and the barbed wire fences around its flower gardens.

The two male nurses led him in, the yellow autumn sunshine lighting up the grey outer walls of the place.

In the yard he stopped. They tried to pull him on.

'See,' he said. 'Won't you believe me? See, I have no shadow. You two have shadows, but I have none.'

The one man looked sideways at his companion. He said nothing then, but turned and walked quickly back to the big gate. The other man followed him.

Outside they looked back once, through the bars of the gate.

The yard of the asylum looked very bright and empty in the mellow autumn sunshine.

It Was the Smell

It was the smell he noticed first. It seemed to be coming out from the inside of the hospital with every turn of the big revolving doors. Out and over him, so that standing there in the sunshine, all the memories of pain he ever knew came back to him. The dentist and the soft whirr of the drill heating the tooth and then prodding on into the soft inside. And the time when he had torn the skin on the back of his hand, in the smithy, and the village doctor had put in the stitches, pushing the flabby skin to get the needle through. The time too when he had been to this place before, when they had done the things to his arm just after the horse had kicked him. They'd told him that perhaps he'd have to come again, to stay a little while.

And so he was back. The private hire car which had brought him was now driving away and the urge came to run after it, to ride away to Megan and the gentle ones at home.

A porter came out of the small green hut at the bottom of the steps. A rounded fatted little man with a grey woollen cardigan showing as he buttoned up his blue double-breasted uniform, the brass buttons glinting in the winter sunshine.

'Hullo,' said the porter. Little kind wrinkles formed around his eyes as he smiled at Glyn. 'Visitor or patient?'

'Patient, sir.'

Even as he said it Glyn knew that it was wrong, to say sir to this little man.

'What ward, sir?' asked the porter, the gentle eyes still smiling, no more, no less.

'Male One,' said Glyn.

'Come with me, I'll show you the way.'

Inside the corridor the smell seemed to go. In there with the trolleys moving along with a little squeak sometimes from their rubber wheels on the polished floor. The patients lying there sometimes looked up at Glyn and the porter as they passed by, raising their heads to stare anxiously, and then falling flat on the stretchers again.

A woman's voice came speaking carefully over the loud-speaker system, asking for a Dr Jones. The name echoed up the long reaches of the green corridor, Dr Jones, Dr Jones . . . Just like that posh hotel up in Glasgow where he and Megan had spent their honeymoon and where they had always been paging someone.

The corridor seemed to be so very long, for the ends seemed to meet. Those days at the technical school where he had learnt draughtsmanship so that he could try to be a better blacksmith than Father. There they'd told him that parallel lines appear to meet. He turned to the little man.

'Seem to meet, don't they?'

The man looked up at him, his mouth a little open, but his eyes still smiling.

'What sir?'

'The walls,' and Glyn pointed with his left hand down the corridor.

The porter nodded, and then, 'We're here, sir.'

They turned down a side corridor, with white doors on either side, all the way. They stopped before one with a little notice, SISTER.

'Here sir,' said the little man. 'They'll receive you in here.'

Then came the shaving.

They placed screens around his bed, closing him off from the others lying in the ward. The whiteness and the closeness frightened him and he wanted to push them spinning away on their wheels. They placed the screens end to end around the enamelled bed so that he could only see the green walls of the ward over the top. And at the bottom, in the space between the floor and the metal of the screen, he sometimes saw the black shoes and woollen stockings of a nurse, stark against the whiteness of the screens.

A man came in between two of the screens, drawing them together after him. He was rolling up the sleeves of a white coat and in his hand he had a small black case. Glyn thought at first that this was it, that the time had come. But as the man put his bag on the bed, Glyn saw that there were little areas of dirt at the ends of his hairy bony fingers. This then could not be the doctor, for always in school at the Clean Hands Campaign they had told him how such men had spotless hands and nails.

'I've come to shave you,' said the man. 'To prep you.'

The barber stripped back the bedclothes. And then using an ether soap he lathered all the hair on Glyn's chest, under his arms and on the nape of his neck. Even the hair on the back of his shoulder blades.

Lying there on his face among the pillows Glyn could feel the soft scrape as the man shaved off the soft silky hairs from his body.

When it was all over, Glyn sat up and looked at his body, white and soft with the dark roots of the hairs showing black against his skin.

'Why?' he asked. 'Why do you do this?'

'Germs, germs love to cling to hair. Meat and drink to them.'

And with that the barber went. Soon afterwards they moved the screens to the next bed and Glyn heard the little murmur from there as the man worked.

That night there was a little pink tablet. And a long fine needle stinging his arm. With the sleep that followed came strange dreams, full of desire, and of fulfilment.

There was redness in his vision. Until he at last opened his eyes, painfully and very slowly.

Even the quiet light of the ward hurt him, so that he shut his eyes quickly before seeing much except the whiteness at the bottom of the bed.

There was the pain too. Down his back and along the side of his thighs. As after that day when he had first used the heavy striking hammer for his father, all day.

The redness became slowly blacker as he lay there. But the pain . . . Perhaps a little movement of his leg would ease it. In the blackness of his mind he could see Megan too, a far-away picture, small like the polyphotos she had once taken. But across the view came little flashes of red, like lightning, zigzagging fast across. Perhaps it was all because of the pain? If perhaps he moved his body she would come nearer, clearer?

He moved his one leg a little. Suddenly all became dazzling white, with sometimes flashes of red, now sharp pointed and hitting straight for the centre of his head . . .

When he next awoke he opened his eyes straight away, but his body felt numb and stiff as after a long awkward sleep.

There were the two of them at the bottom of the bed. A man in white and a nurse. The man with a small silver instrument swinging in his fingers.

They were watching him. The man calmly and with interest, the nurse with a little curious smile on her pale lips.

'Feeling better?' asked the man, dropping the silver instrument into a pocket of his white overall.

Glyn tried to nod but his neck was stiff and would not bend.

The doctor turned to the nurse.

'I don't think he's noticed yet. Perhaps he's not out yet.'

The nurse nodded.

'Perhaps not, doctor.'

But Glyn had heard. And with their words it all came back to him. Why he was here. And from somewhere deep inside him a whole rush of pity was loosed.

He must not cry, must not show his tears to these two who were watching.

But it was not until he tried to knuckle back the tears that he knew for certain that they had taken away his arm.

Robert

The doors had been painted last summer, and from where he was working in the potato garden he could see their green, brighter than the level lawn in front of the doctor's quarters, away to his left.

There, on his right, the square red building with the painted doors, in the corner of the long garden.

The first day he'd come to the institution they'd put him to work in the gardens. He'd been a little dazed then. The death of his wife, and after that they'd come to take him away. The stripping naked in the tiled washroom, and the shower bath. And after that the hose squirting out strong-smelling disinfectant into the thick matted hair under his arms and on his body. A hose held by a uniformed man who handled the shining brass nozzle like a fireman. Pointing it at the old, rather bent yellow body shivering there against the white tiles. All in the first few days, the change and the rough food. The rows of them sleeping in the ward at night.

Robert had been dazed at first. And he had thought that the building was the tool-shed for the gardens. Until the man with the wooden leg who worked with him, told him. Told him simply and quietly. The wooden peg of his leg sinking into the soft soil as they stood to talk.

'That's the mort, Robert, where we'll lie someday.'

But the idea hadn't frightened him. For he knew that he had come here to die. And every day as he worked, he became used to seeing the trolley moving from the sick wards, through the potatoes, and up to the green doors. At first he used to stop work, stare a little, and then lower his head as the trolley passed, quiet on its pneumatic wheels. But the others kept on working, and after a time he, too, carried on.

Almost every day a hearse would draw up. The driver would get out and call a porter. Then they'd carry in the empty shell of a coffin. Carry it lightly between them. After a time they'd come out again. Robert could see by the way they bent that the coffin was heavy. That it was full.

When the strangeness had worn away, he accepted the life of the institution quite calmly. Became, with the rest of the old men, a part of it. But one thing worried him. That which he had seen the first day out in the gardens. The bright green of the doors . . .

When Robert first saw the little girl he knew that she was connected in some vague way with the one disquiet thing in his life.

She was the daughter of the matron. The first time he saw her was when she was playing ball on the lawn outside the doctor's house. She had a rounded bat in her hand and she was bouncing the ball against the wall. Then a window opened in the ivy-covered wall and a maid called out, 'Ruth, don't you dare break a window.'

Away among the straight rows of the potatoes, Robert could hear as she answered back – 'Don't care.'

Then she started to bounce the ball on the lawn. A hard hit and then the ball was away among the dark ridges of the garden.

'Get my ball.'

He slowly straightened his back, one foot and one hand on the spade. Looked at her a second before he answered.

'Yes, little girl, I'll get your ball.'

Taking his spade Robert moved up and down the rows sweeping the green pliable stems aside as he searched for the ball. It took him long to find it and little girl kept calling from the other side of the box hedge – 'Hurry, old man. Hurry up and throw me back my ball.'

At last he found it, and with a gentle under-arm throw he pitched it to her. He heard her calling out to thank him, and then she was on with her game again.

His old and tired eyes couldn't see her too well and so he left his spade among the potatoes, the handle sticking up to mark its position. And then he crossed over to the edge of the low hedge, beyond which the little girl was playing.

The back of her hair he saw first, the long yellow hair bouncing off her neck as she jumped around after the ball.

From her hair his eyes travelled slowly down her back. The gay printed frock with the red and blue flowers on it.

And then he saw it . . .

The thin band around her waist, neat and narrow, tightly buckled at the one side.

The belt was green.

*

Often after that he saw her playing in the grounds. Sometimes she was pushing a little pram with a stiff dolly sitting upright in it. Pushing the pram slowly through the clogging gravel of the garden paths. At other times she would be leading a little dog on its lead. Holding him back as he dragged her on.

Whenever he heard her coming he would move up until he could see her quite plainly. It was her thin high voice he always heard first. He wished his eyes were better. Time was when he could see every snare that he had laid in the dull light of a summer dawn. But now . . .

As he would move up to her his eyes focused for one thing only.

The green belt.

Robert knew that one day soon he must die in the institution. The talk in the wards every evening was always of that. That was a certainty. The only unknown thing was, how long yet they would have to dig the gardens or scrub the corridors.

And so Robert made his plans.

After many weeks of watching he knew that the little girl went to tea every Friday to the house of the doctor. On her way she passed through a small length of the path where the box hedges had been allowed to grow high. A few yards of path only, where all was quiet and unseen.

Robert waited there one Friday afternoon.

The two porters held on firmly to his arms as they led him through the gardens.

Just inside the main gate the ambulance was waiting, the steel bars dark against the tinted windows.

As the three walked along, Robert sagged a little so that the two uniformed men had to hold him up and jerk him along.

But passing the back of the mortuary he straightened up, and spoke. But without looking at either of the two men.

'That's the mort; it's got green doors.'

'Yes, Robert, it has; come along now.'

And they jerked him on.

Robert spoke again.

'Do you know what's behind them?'

The one porter looked at the other, and just then Robert called out, suddenly very loud.

The driver of the van by the gate looked up, startled. And for the remaining yards up to the ambulance, one of the attendants kept his one hand tight over Robert's mouth.

They locked him in and watched the van drive quickly away.

'What a dirty old man,' said the one. 'Always so quiet too.'

'Ay,' said the other. 'Poor little Ruth, you never can tell.'

Only a Green Shutter

The two small girls stood gravely, side by side, on the worn stones of the old quay. Behind them the grey houses of the seaside town rose, terrace upon terrace, to the hard blue sky of the summer's day. In front, shaking a little on the ebbing tide, was the small beautifully white ship. Beyond stretched the sea, its surface touched in places by the colours of gay craft, and disturbed to a foamy whiteness where swimmers laughed and played.

It was the girl who had the long pigtails of fair hair who said, without looking at her friend but staring at the white sides of the small ship,

'I think this one has come from somewhere ever so far away.'

'From outer space, Jenny?' asked the other little girl. She had dark, short-cut hair and held a dripping ice lolly in her hand.

The fair-haired little girl shook her head and put her hands in the pockets of her jeans as she answered, thoughtfully,

'Oh no, Susan Ann, just from Jamaica.'

'Why Jamaica?' asked Susan Ann as she took a slow, deliberately large lick of the lolly. She paused, wiped a drip from the point of her small chin and then went on, slowly, 'Why Jamaica, Jenny?'

'White ships, so my Daddy told me this morning, white ships so he said come always from Jamaica. There's heaps and heaps of white paint there, Susan Ann.'

'Oh,' answered Susan Ann, and prepared to attack her ice lolly again.

They didn't say very much more to one another, but watched the distant swimmers; the passing boats; and the slow heaving rhythm of the white little ship which was so near to them.

It was when Susan Ann had finished her lolly and had dropped the smooth, white, empty stick over the railings of the quayside into the sea water that she said, 'Jenny, I know a boy who saw a ship which had come from Jamaica.'

'Where?'

'Up on the coast, on a Friday. It was a white ship. And he threw a stone on its deck, and do you know what?'

'No, what Susan Ann?'

'Well, up came two pirates, ready for fighting.'

'Sure?'

'Sure and certain.'

'Oh.'

Jenny put up a hand and pulled a wisp of her fair hair down over her blue eyes. She waited for the wind off the sea to blow it up again, and then she felt in the pockets of her jeans and said, 'I used to keep a stone in each of my pockets, but they got heavy.'

'And hurt when you fall, don't they?'

'Yes.'

Susan Ann made a little toss of her hand towards the white ship, and she said, 'It would be easy to throw a stone and fetch up a pirate from Jamaica.'

'I'd love to see one.'

'Let's.'

Both children turned rapidly and ran from the quayside to a path which went up the hot, sun-drenched cliff. They each picked up a stone, and Susan Ann said happily, 'A big one for you and a little one for me. I'm sure it's the right sort of spell.'

Jenny answered, 'What sort of stone did the boy say he had?'

'Didn't say. Doesn't much matter though.'

They went back to the quay, past the white wooden seats of the town; past the small shops selling dried fish and hats of coloured plaited straw. They walked more carefully, as if both were afraid that the ship might have sensed their plan and sailed on to the freedom of the seas. But all was well; the ship still lifted and fell a little. And the colour of the summer sea was reflected in a touch of blueness under her stern.

'Who first?' asked Jenny.

Susan hesitated a moment: 'Both together, I think.'

They tiptoed right up to the quayside railings and stood side by side, each holding their stones.

'I'll count three,' said Susan Ann.

'Right.'

'One, two . . . three.'

Together the two small girls heaved each her stone through the clear warm air and onto the planking of the deck of the white ship. One stone fell just behind the well; the other hit the brass coping of the cabin skylight.

After the two dull thuds of the falling stones there was a silence.

'Good thing nobody was watching,' said Jenny.

'Hope the two pirates are coming,' answered Susan Ann.

And then, quite abruptly, there was the sound of scuffling from the inside of the cabin.

'Oh,' said Susan Ann. 'Oh, they really are coming.'

Jenny backed away from the edge of the quay and Susan Ann, after a moment, moved too. And then the cabin door flung open and two men came out. The one, an oldish man in dirty white trousers and a sailor's jersey came first up the steps. Behind him, and grabbing towards him, was a great, thin, wiry man dressed in a dirty dull-buttoned uniform. He carried a small knife, with a handle made of white plastic.

The older man seemed to be wanting to escape for, once up the steps, he crouched behind the coping of the cabin skylights. The man in the dirty uniform stood at the top of the steps, balancing the white knife in his brown hands. Then the older man suddenly seemed to decide to make a fast-running leap from the edge of the white ship to the safety of the quay railings. He sprang through the warm clean air. Out at sea there were the shouts of the happy bathers and the distant beat of outboard engines.

And, as the man leapt over the space above the ebbing water, the other man in the dirty uniform threw the white-handled knife he was holding so casually. Both children heard the whine of the steel in the air; and heard the dull thud as it landed in the back of the elder man even as he reached out at the end of his leap and held onto the railings. He clung to the rusty iron for a moment with one hand, his other hand reaching around trying to pluck out the knife from his back. A moment like that and then he fell, softly and surely into the fast blue water rushing out to sea.

The man in the dirty old uniform came to the side of the ship from the top of the steps and looked down. And then he looked up, for he suddenly seemed to sense the presence of Jenny and Susan Ann on the other side of the quay. He stared at them both for a moment, and then he took in a short sharp breath and he said, 'How long have *you* been there?'

It was Susan Ann who answered: 'Ever since we threw the two stones onto the deck of the ship and called out you two pirates.'

Jenny went on, 'You are from Jamaica, aren't you?'

The man in the dirty old uniform looked down at the tide-race, and then looked out to the bay where all was innocence. After a while he said, 'Yes, we both were pirates. Pirates from Jamaica. He stole my treasure and I killed him.'

'Pirates always do that, don't they?' called Susan Ann.

The man only nodded and it was left for Jenny to say, 'Pirates always take revenge on a traitor.'

And, after a little silence, Susan Ann said, 'They kill even their best friends, if they have to.'

The man echoed, 'If they have to, yes.'

He was staring at the two small girls and it seemed as if he sensed some of that ruthlessness and innocence which pervade all children. He seemed to sense that they approved of what he had done; that he was part of the cast of an essential make-believe.

After a little time Susan Ann said, 'We must go home.'

The man, still standing on the edge of the white boat, said quietly, 'You'll not tell anyone that you saw two pirates from Jamaica this afternoon?'

'Oh no,' answered Susan Ann.

'And if we did, no one would believe us, would they?' went on Jenny.

The man looked sadly at them as he answered, 'Grown-ups never believe such things.'

Susan Ann and Jenny turned then and ran home. Once, as they entered an alley between the tall, pastel-coloured houses, they both stopped and looked back the far way down to the quay.

The tall man in the dirty uniform was still standing on the edge of the white ship. He was looking down at the water, his head a little on one side, listening rather than watching.

Susan Ann said, 'Next time we see a white boat, we'll throw *three* stones onto it, and *three* pirates from Jamaica will come.'

'Don't be silly,' answered Jenny. 'Don't be silly, three would make a poor fight. It'd have to be two like today, or twenty, to be really exciting. But come on, I've found money in the deep corner of my jeans' pocket. We'll share broken candy on the way home.'

The south wind off the sea intensified a little and shook a broken green shutter on its one rusty hinge high above them. The clatter frightened them far more than anything they had seen or heard that summer's day, and they ran home holding hands all the way. They arrived home breathless and frightened; everyone laughed when Susan Ann and Jenny told them about the terrible noise from the broken green shutter.

The Hedgehog

Dafydd dangled his legs over the back of the two-wheeled hay-cart, stretching with the tips of his school boots to reach the low-cut grass of the hayfield. His one hand holding tight to one of the corner poles and his other hand sweeping the wooden floorboards at the back of him. For behind him were all the insects from the past loads of hay, running about on the wood. Brown, fast-moving earwigs and lots of black-and-yellow beetles.

'Dad,' he called, 'Ride me over a haycock to give me a bounce.'

His father paused the horse a moment and rubbed the sweaty mane on her neck.

'Think of Bess here, lad. Tired she is and this field we want to clear before tonight. Besides, Dafydd, time it is that you were in bed. Your mother has just gone to put the little one to sleep.'

'Oh, go on, Dad. Bump me over a haycock. Fun it is to be almost thrown over the back. And Dad, how it shakes all these beetles up.'

Edwards Llys jerked on the horse again and then let his arm fall to his side as Bess walked on. Little and stumpy was Edwards Llys. Indeed, for many years, Edwards Stump he had been. But Edwards had turned rough on any man who said Stump in his hearing. And so it was that with time the Stump had been forgotten and when he came to the llys from the smallholding, Edwards Llys he naturally became.

The haymaking this year had been easy. The hot sun had dried the hay in a couple of days and there was the danger that unless the hay was carried tonight, that overdone it would be. Last night he and Mag had raked the hay into long rows. Handy with a rake was the wife. And this morning as soon as the dew had risen, they had cocked the hay into neat little bundles all over the field. Dafydd had helped too, while the little one lay under the shadow of the big alder tree, by the pool. Dafydd had his little short pitchfork and his Dad had spurred him on with the talk of the man who had once got the steel prongs of his fork red-hot with the heat of the working.

And all the afternoon they had been carrying in the hay into the Dutch barn, a galvanised iron roof on high steel pillars, by the side of the stone farmhouse. The woman doing the loading and Edwards pitching up the hay to her, she making a load of the hay with her bare hands. And ever looking from the top of the hay to the pool where the little one lay sleeping.

It was there among the nettles and the long, uncut grass that he found it. Rolled up very tightly and lying very still in the grass.

Dafydd raised one foot very carefully and rolled the hedgehog over.

Then came the idea. The wonderful, wonderful idea.

His father was pitching hay on the far side of the wagon and his mother was on her knees among the hay. And so there was no one to watch him.

Taking off his jacket Dafydd placed it over the top of the hedgehog. Then he buttoned up the coat and carried it all by the sleeves towards the barn. Holding his jacket from him, for the spines came through the worn tweed of the jacket and threatened his knees.

To the barn. And then carefully up the ladder to the top of the stack. Struggle it was to get himself and the hedgehog up, but at last he managed it.

There, in the centre of the haystack was the hole. When starting the stack his dad had filled a sack with hay, packing it tightly. Then he had built the stack all around this, pulling the sack up all the time as the hay rose higher. And so the chimney was formed in the middle of the stack. So that the hay could 'sweat'.

The sack was out of the chimney now. Lying to the one side.

Over by the hole, Dafydd shook out the hedgehog onto the top of the hay. Then with the toe of his boot he rolled it over the side of the hole. The dull plop as the animal hit the ground at the bottom of the stack.

He was peering over the darkness of the hole when he heard his mother calling, 'Dafydd, Dafydd, where are you? Answer me. Where are you? Answer me, boy.'

'Here, Mam, I am. On top of the stack.'

She was climbing the ladder now, her feet slipping in her hurry.

'Oh, you naughty, naughty boy. What did your dad tell you?'

Dafydd was putting on his jacket.

'Not to climb the stack, Mam.'

'Then why did you do it, Dafydd? Why did you do it?'

She was on the hay and her arms swinging and her shoulders twitching, her face red with the running and the climbing. A strand of her long black hair, full of hayseeds, fell across her face. She halted one arm to throw it back. Then over she came to the boy and stood by him, her one hand pointing down into the blackness of the chimney.

'That big black hole. What if you should slip in, Dafydd?'

He looked down at the blackness and up to the red face of his mother.

'Yes, Mam.'

Then quite suddenly she threw her arms around him and dragged him to the ladder. And when they reached the bottom her husband was there.

But although he had already cut a hazel stick from the hedge she would not leave him touch the boy. And so Edwards went off to unharness the horse, for they would unload the hay in the morning.

And Mam took him to the house, holding tight to his shoulder all the way.

Lying in his little iron bedstead that night Dafydd could not sleep. The enamel of the iron was peeling off and the ironwork felt hot to his sweaty palms.

And there was the moonlight. The little one, too, sleeping there in the cot in the corner was making sucking noises and he could hear the bubbles forming on her lips.

He'd kicked off all the clothes now and the last he could remember before sleep came was the slight draught from the chimney cooling the bottoms of his feet.

But he awoke soon, for the dream had been dreadful. The spikes there had been driving into him. And his Mam had been in the dream trying to push away the spikes. His Dad had been in it too, laughing there in the distance. When he awoke he could still feel the pain in his flesh and rubbing his hot body he was surprised to find his skin whole and damp only with the sweat, and not with blood.

Lying on his side he could see out and into the yard. Out through the little square panes of the old-fashioned glass. The unpainted galvanised iron roof of the hay barn was shining very bright in the moonlight. Dad had said that he was going to paint it as soon as the hay was in. Said too, that perhaps he should help him.

Watching the bright gleam of the iron sheeting, the spines and the dream came back to him. So that he could not stand the darkness and the breathing of the little one. He slid off the bed and went across to the open windows, looking out over the apple trees and towards the hay.

It was his mother he awakened. She sat up with a little grunt when he shook her bare shoulder.

'What is it? What's wrong?'

And then Dafydd spoke.

'It's only me, Mam, me.'

'You, Dafydd, what's wrong? Why do you come to our bedroom at this time of the night?'

'Oh, Mam—'

'Quiet now boy, or wake your father you will and he's tired what with the haymaking. Now, shush, now and tell me all what's wrong.'

He told her all. All about how he had caught the hedgehog and dropped it down the hole in the stack.

'And oh, Mam, I want to get it out again and put it back where it belongs, back among the nettles, Mam.'

Lying there with the lad whispering it worried her. For it might have been the boy himself, or the little one.

The thought of it worked upon her so that she suddenly stopped patting Dafydd and turned over and shook her husband.

He rolled over towards her, throwing out a long arm. She caught it in mid-air and by jerking his elbow joint, she awoke him. And told him.

He was annoyed at first. Said that the lad wanted a damn good lathering to stop him treating animals so.

But in the end he got up.

And she rose and dressed herself and Dafydd and the three of them went to the haystack.

At the bottom of the ladder Edwards pointed to the height.

'Hopeless it is. Thirteen foot deep that hole is, Mag. Devil must have been in Dafydd to do this. Wait here you two.'

He went away to the tool-shed under the big apple tree and came back with the electric lamp from his bicycle and a length of cord. Under his one arm he carried the long pole with the net on the end of it. Patent this was, for picking apples from the top branches of the trees where a ladder could not reach. By pulling a lever at the end of the pole the mouth of the net was closed. And he brought too, the leather mittens which he used to press the thorns down when patching a hedge.

He climbed the ladder. She followed after, carrying the lad with her.

'Hold the boy back from the hole, Mag, one down there's enough.'

She held Dafydd around the chin, cupping her palm under his jaw. Edwards fastened the lamp to the end of the cord. Then he dropped the lamp down, peering over the edge of the hole.

'Animal is there. But dead it sure will be what with all the heat at the bottom of the hole. Devil was sure with you when you did this thing, lad.'

Then he dropped the pole with the net at the end. Holding it with his one hand, and with his other angling the cord to light up the bottom of the hole.

Then he clicked the lever.

'Got it.'

The three of them climbed down to the grass of the orchard again.

There, in the moonlight, Edwards put on his leather mittens and took out gently the hedgehog from the net.

It was still rolled up.

Edwards touched a spine with a leather finger.

'Think that alive it is. They do say that these things unroll when dead. But stand still, we'll see.'

For a full two minutes they stood there, the hedgehog lying quiet in the light of the lamp.

Then slowly, very slowly, it began to unroll a little. And then its head came slowly out and the back became more flat.

Not a word they said but stood there, watching. And then it began to move away into the shadows of the apple trees. Moving away slowly out of the circle of light of the torch.

Even when it had gone away they stood there. Until Edwards clicked off the light and said: 'Catch our death of cold we will, out at night. Back to our beds the three of us, for the hedgehog is alive and well.'

And with that they went in.

But upstairs Edwards whispered to his wife. And she came in and carried away the cot, with the little one sleeping in it. Carried it away and put it by the side of their double bed.

But Dafydd was glad. For he could sleep now, with the hedgehog safe. And not even the bubbles from the mouth of the little one to trouble him.

About the Author

Cledwyn Hughes was an Anglo-Welsh author of short stories, novels, and narrative non-fiction. He wrote for more than 30 years across a wide range of genres including crime, 'Celtic Noir', children's and topographical writing.

Born in Llansantffraid, Montgomeryshire, he worked as a hospital pharmacist in the north of England before settling down in Wales to write full-time. His work has been featured in magazines such as *Suspense*, as well as in collections like Woodrow Wyatt's *English Stories*. He was also a regular contributor to the BBC.

He is best known for the novel *The Civil Strangers* (1950) and the macabre novella *The Inn Closes for Christmas* (1947), which remained in print until shortly before his untimely death. His contemporaries called him a 'brilliant young Welshman whose short stories have already established his reputation' (*The Spectator*).

Dear Reader,

We'd love your attention for one more page to tell you about the crisis in children's reading, and what we can all do.

Studies have shown that reading for fun is the **single biggest predictor of a child's future life chances** – more than family circumstance, parents' educational background or income. It improves academic results, mental health, wealth, communication skills, ambition and happiness.[1]

The number of children reading for fun is in rapid decline. Young people have a lot of competition for their time. In 2024, 1 in 10 children and young people in the UK aged 5 to 18 did not own a single book at home.[2]

Hachette works extensively with schools, libraries and literacy charities, but here are some ways we can all raise more readers:

- Reading to children for just 10 minutes a day makes a difference
- Don't give up if children aren't regular readers – there will be books for them!
- Visit bookshops and libraries to get recommendations
- Encourage them to listen to audiobooks
- Support school libraries
- Give books as gifts

There's a lot more information about how to encourage children to read on our website: **www.RaisingReaders.co.uk**

Thank you for reading.

hachette
UK

---

[1] OECD, '21st-Century Readers: Developing Literacy Skills in a Digital World', 2021, https://www.oecd.org/en/publications/21st-century-readers_a83d84cb-en.html

[2] National Literacy Trust, 'Book Ownership in 2024', November 2024, https://literacytrust.org.uk/research-services/research-reports/book-ownership-in-2024